The Last Great Inquisition: It will Rain Today

(or the boring title)

An Introvert's Guide to Happiness and the Quieting Discontent of the Mind.

– A coming of age tale

By Adam Patterson

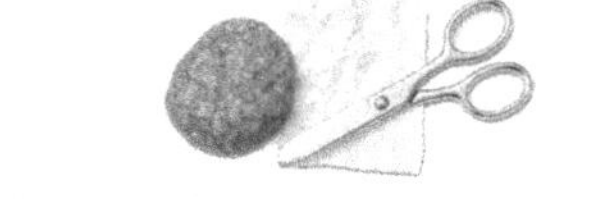

RPSS Publishing - Buffalo, New York

RPSSPublishing.com

The Last Great Inquisition: It will Rain Today

- Perfect Bound

ISBN: 978-1-956688-70-2

Printed in the United States of America

10 9 8 7 6 5 4 3 2 1

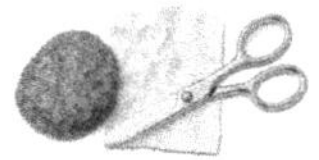

RPSS Publishing - Buffalo, New York

When an angel shows up on Texas's door to announce the apocalypse and ruin her happy plan for life, she has to seek God, who has locked himself away in the closet, to stop the battling demons and angels along the way.

AND THEN:

This is the Beginning bit

"O God, I could be bounded in a nutshell and count myself a king of infinite space, were it not that I have bad dreams."

[Hamlet Act 2 Scene 2]

Her name was Texas, not after the state but the food. She wore her red hair up in a bun and a pair of blue glasses that kept sliding off her nose, while her slippers slipped and slopped as she paced the room. Her mug of hot chocolate had cooled to a nice July morning. They said the chocolate would help serotonin, but it wasn't working. The baggy white shirt rustled as she moved around, and the sweatpants kept falling down.

She opened her laptop and started a game, then turned it off. She opened it up and started searching, shut it again. She stood up, squeezed her fists, and paced some more.

The letter was on her desk. It was on her desk and there. A wave of heat and heaviness settled on her shoulder, and tears formed in the corners of her eyes. It was still on the desk.

She stared a bit longer, pressing her thumb against her teeth.

She picked up the letter and put it down. Walked to the fridge downstairs, nothing new since twenty minutes ago. Grabbed cheese and took a bite, then made a sandwich but abandoned it halfway through, and finally grabbed an apple, but one bite in, she decided not to. Her mother emerged from the stairs.

"Texas, dear, what are you doing up?"

"Nothing," Texas said, gripping the railing, heading back up.

"Mmmm." The girl's mom said thoughtfully. "Maybe you should pray on it."
"What!?" Texas stood up straight. "No, mom. I'll figure it out." And with that, she ducked back upstairs.

In her room, she glanced again at her desk, opened up the letter from the consortium Alhomberus, Tesetol, Lax, Amberdeen, and Santiago. Congratulations, you've been accepted to the internship. Arrive...

She paced again, the cheese wasn't sitting right and dashed to the bathroom. One, two, three, flushes later she removed her head and a clear reflection came through. "What are you doing?" She asked herself. And once more, her head entered the rim of the toilet to expel the last of her stomach's contents. But, this time it hurt.

She heaved again. There was something in her throat that was stuck, something hard, long, tasted like copper. And her stomach pushed once more, squeezing and heaving something small and metallic.

She pushed the last of her breath, and from her mouth was birthed a key. It was just a little key, no bigger than a pinky, with an unlocky bit at one end and a holdy bit at the other. It bore no markings or name and was as unremarkable as plain toast.

"Uuhem" were herm's first words. It was a dark and heavy word that carried weight, causing Texas's shoulders to slump and her hands to crinkle. There was a bulk upon her chest as she slowly turned to see herm standing in the door frame.

Herm was a glowing figure, translucent in nature, with long hair. Herm began again, "Hello, my name is Gabby, I'm your guardian angel, and I'm here to herald the end of the world."

"What?" Texas sputtered, losing ground on footing while kneeling on the floor, and space/time turned in while still contained in the tiny bathroom.

"Nope, there is no way around it." Herm's voice lightened, but the tightness in her chest hugged each rib.

Texas checked her pulse, good. She smelled the air, no burned toast, good. She asked another question, "I don't understand." Nope, that was a statement.

"You asked a question..." Were herm's last word before the night took her, and with that, Texas melted to the floor and pressed her tired face against the cold tile

The First Bit

"And this was their appearance: they had a human likeness, but each had four faces, and each of them had four wings. Their legs were straight, and the soles of their feet were like the sole of a calf's foot. And they sparkled like burnished bronze. Under their wings on their four sides, they had human hands. And the four had their faces and their wings thus."-

[Ezekiel 1:5-8]

Somewhere between Steele and Jamestown, North Dakota, a hundred miles south of Fessenden in the middle of the flat lands, spotted with lakes, sits the town of Nowhere (pronounced NOwhere), North Dakota. A place so flat people would ask, "How flat was she?" And invariably there would be a crude joke of a small-chested woman, or cows that could never run off, or children who never stopped rolling downhill because once you started moving down the curve of the earth, you couldn't stop until you ended where you started.

Texas knew it as home, and as the sun cracked on the horizon, spilling the yoke of morning's dew upon blades of starved grass, she woke up to the shrilling sound of a trumpet playing, wholly out of tune, whaling upon her head from somewhere within her house. Hoping it was the remnants of a dream, she sat up from the bathroom floor and thought nothing of it. She stood up and looked in the mirror; her hair was still a dirty mess of fiery snarls on a porcelain complexion, and though she didn't cry as much as she used to when she was a baby, her disposition hadn't changed. There was a sadness about her; it was the quiet kind. There was always a smile and a laugh; it was what was expected of her.

She tried to remember last night, but it was fuzzy. There was panic, fear, and a dose of cheese. She took a step back, and her heel kicked something that made a ting sound against the porcelain tub. It was the key, unremarkable as before, unadorned as her, and perfectly plain.

Texas bundled her hair in a ponytail, put on her blue-rimmed glasses, and made her way out.

She stood in the doorway of her bedroom and looked around her pedestrian habitation and grinned. She knew there was someone with her last night. A male? Fred? She went from the hallway back to the bathroom in four steps, putting the toothbrush in her mouth and sitting on the toilet for a morning break. Then a thought came into her head, one that makes its way in every morning, like a mugger taking that sense of morning calm, her sense of place.

She thought about the letter from last night, which was clear. There was what was expected of her. Go to college, get a job, have a family, die, etc. It was all neatly laid out for her. It was simple, really, live in the in-between bits, be disappointed because the moments of excitement were not continuous. And move on to some partner, procreate or adopt, and die. But it always ends in death ~ the answer to life is always death. If you could grow up to be anything you want to be, then surely you can grow up to be nothing? No need for thoughts now.

She finished up in the bathroom and opened the door to find a thin, dark adolescent about her age, slightly leaning forward. He squeezed the three books in his hands.

"What was I reading? Right? That's what you were going to ask? Grabbed a couple of titles from Mary's forbidden section. I remember how much you liked the forbidden section. I thought I could read these, and you'd stop by the coffee shop, and we could... You know... talk to something." He wasn't reading the cues. "Did you have plans today??" Fred rambled and closed his eyes. He noticed she wasn't wearing a bra. Icy water. Grandma, not his grandma, a grandma, the kind without teeth and a gnarled mole. Chipmunks. Layers of blue blankets and a scented soap on top. He kept his thoughts swirling.

"I didn't." Texas leaned against the door frame. "Ah, Henrick Cornelius Agrippa. A little light reading, some Neoplatonism." She said, reading the titles. "You haven't been around in a while." It had been 2 weeks since he stopped by asking to borrow a book. It had been three weeks since she stopped into his family's coffee shop. It's lonely in a small town.

"Yes, I like him, that Neoplatonism. So, you like him? Huh, we like the same author.

What are the odds?"

"Not a person." Texas mocked. Fred squinted. Texas realized its current state. "Keep your eyes closed." Texas said as she moved around him and into her room, shutting the door behind her.

"Ah..." There was a long pause. He opened his eyes, "So, what are you doing today?" "I don't know, Fred. Kind of creepy that you are here this early. Were you waiting for me outside the bathroom? Because that would be weird."

"No, that would be silly... I'm here... you know... cause I get things. Book. I have books, I get them. I got them. Yes. We could read them together." Pause. Regroup. "You want to go to the pond? That's what I meant. You know, I was thinking it would be a beautiful day, maybe we could go for a walk or something?"

She opened the door properly dressed, "We'll see." Rolling her eyes, the glasses fell from her nose.

"I'm going to miss you when you leave." Fred said on her heels.

Texas stopped and took a breath. "I don't think I'm going to leave." There she said it. It felt good.

His heart skipped, "really..." with a smile. "I thought your boss got you that summer program at his company, like a really hard-to-find, great internship. How did you pull that off?"

"I just clean his house; I've only talked to him once." She paused, "Besides, he wouldn't even give me a letter of recommendation to his company. Just said I'd have to apply."

"Oh," Fred stopped. Ruffling his feathers, "When I make it big and have a lot of money, you can come and work for me..." Fred blushed, "or something like that. I mean I'd give you a lot of money, not like make you work for it... That came out wrong."

"I've never been interested in money," Texas reminded him. She took a breath and looked at her room. "Yeah, well, I mean I have to work today, but we'll see." she said plainly, gazing at the bedroom mirror, and in a moment of quiet, she looked herself in the eye. Why am I even working entered her mind. Then a horn blared, raking its melody across her mind. "What is that sound!"

Fred peered back, "Mary, brought some stranger home after her morning constitutional." "Why?"

"I don't know, probably another homeless person she wants to feed or-- hey, happy Shelling Day." Fred said.

Texas leaned her head against the door frame, looking into her little world.

"Don't remind me."

"I completely forgot!" Fred ran up, dropped the books, and hugged her. He closed his eyes and mouthed Grandma to himself. And once again the trumpet sounded.

"I'm going to murder someone this morning." Texas said quietly, shrugging off Fred. "Who plays a trumpet at 8 am and I'm here, in the hallway rather than in my bed?"

The trumpet blared again as if to warn against rocks ahead. "Fine." Texas threw her hands up and made her way to the stairs.

The trumpet blared as her foot hit the first step of the stairs, and for a moment, there was a tangible wall; her chest grew heavy, and her lungs were pulled down. A tight constriction took her breath, and her eyes watered from a force pushing them back, and even as the trumpet faded away, there was a weight upon her shoulders. She took another step, and still the sensation continued, squeezing her from her waist up and strangling her neck and eyes. Step by step, she reached the ground, and while the pressure didn't abate, her breath returned to normal, and her feet regained their buoyancy.

Mary, with her grey, silver flecked hair pulled up into a bun, with an old sweater hung loose around her, tilted the frying pan toward her, and with a flick of her wrist, the eggs turned over. She spun to see Texas, in a stars and moon loose-fitting shirt and jeans, her hair pointing this way and that in the back of her ponytail. Mary smiled at Texas's frown and let out a twinkle to brighten her daughter's day. She then followed Texas's gaze to the man she had at her table. Her mind turned. Was it a man or a woman at the table? Herm long hair, soft eyes, dark brown glowing skin, didn't betray a gender and herm's lithe like frame hid any physical tells.

"Another! How wonderful! Hi, if you don't remember, my name is Gabby," herm exclaimed running herm finger up and down on the valves of the horn in herm's hand.

She knew him from last night. Was it a dream? "He's an angel," Mary added.

"Yes! I am an angel." Herm's voice, a soft lilt, quiet and piercing, a walking contradiction herm sounded vaguely like everyone and yet indiscernible. Not at all like last night. Herm put the trumpet back to his mouth and took a breath–

"Wait!" Texas sounded, holding up her hand. "It's 8 am, can we wait until after breakfast, please. And Fred's acting weird again." She shook her head. "Wait, an angel?"

"Aren't you supposed to be a terrible creature? In the bible, they are said to be warriors, fearsome and covered in armor? And eyes. I'm sure you're not one." Fred interjected, descending from the stairs, wincing with a heavy breath.

"Yes, whatever you say." Herm put down the horn and stared unblinkingly.

Mary continued on. "Oh, Gabby, this is Fred. Fred's a loving boy and has a bit of a crush on Texas."

Fred's eyes grew as the blood rushed to his cheeks, and he piped up, "Thanks... Ms.

Mary." He said.

"You two grew up together, you're the only girl he knows his age... it'll fade." Mary reminded Texas, who was frozen with her head tilted back, eyes pointed up.

"I'm right here, Ms. Mary." Fred said as he sat down at the table.

Mary began again, "I'm kind of afraid of you leaving up Texas. Speaking of that, we should have the sex talk, or someone else will, and it won't be as sweet as my talk. Are you sure you want to go out into the great big world? It's not nice to people. People aren't nice to people there... You know what? I'll pray about it."

"Wow, this day is getting better by the minute. And one thing at a time, Mom. Gabby, I have some questions." She said to Gabby and sat down, "And, Mom, what is his... her..."

"Herm, I'm an angel and don't live by your biological rules." Gabby said plainly. "Herm? Like hermaphrodite?" Texas took a glass of water.

"No, I'm gender neutral, but English doesn't have a neuter, I'm not a him and I'm not a her, so I'm a herm"

Texas stared at Mary, eyes pleading for an answer, "Well, I couldn't let herm be out here in the cold! Not when I can make herm a hot breakfast." Mary piped in. Herm's trumpet wasn't working either, so I thought herm could fiddle with it here. But I want to touch on the world again. It is a cruel place, Texas. I was thinking, maybe just stay here for one more year. Or more, you know, at your own pace, love."

"No, focus. Mom, you invited someone into possibly murder us in our sleep. Let's address that first." Texas didn't think she had to explain to her mother stranger danger.

"It was five am, there are no bad people out at five am, only industrious, good-hearted souls." Mary smiled.

Texas reevaluated her position on her mother's education.

"And it was very kind of you," Gabby began, "I miss the old ways of hospitality."

"I should want to leave this house," Texas said to herself, grabbing the teapot from the center of the table and pouring herself a mug. "Ok, I'm ready now. I've been thinking about that, the going out in the world bit. Maybe I do stay here. Continue to clean or maybe work as Fred's family's shop. If they'd have me..."

Fred dropped the books. "YES!" in an almost high-pitched squeak, followed by an equally unreal low, "Yes."

"So, may I stay here for a bit longer if I don't take that summer internship?" Trailing off her words.

Mary smiled and turned. "Whatever you'd like to do. I have prayed about it, so I'm very glad to hear you're not going out into the scary, terrible world. You'll always have a home here. When I was out in the world, it was full of thugs and beasts of all kinds, all manner of strange people. Most of those whom you didn't know were beasts until it was too late. I would love for you to stay; it's a Shelling Day miracle!" Her mother said, bringing over a plate full of cheesy eggs with a cupcake and a candle on top.

"Oh, it's your Shelling Day!?" The androgynous herm gleefully shouted; herm eyes hadn't blinked yet.

"No, it's my adoption day, I would prefer you not call it my Shelling Day, Mom."

"Oh, adoption! How wonderful! Yes, thank you, I didn't know what a Shelling Day was.

You humans love to celebrate! Yes, you do." Effervescently exclaiming, herm eyes fixed on Texas who was being careful not to make contact. "Come, Mary, share tea with us!" Herm said not pulling his gaze from Texas.

Mary put the eggs back on the stove and took a seat next to her daughter, holding her hand. "It is your Shelling Day! Oh, how wonderful. Have you thought of what you want to do?"

"I would like to not call it my Shelling Day."

"It's better than Dumpster Day." Fred said, and Mary shot him a look while making his way into the kitchen. "Anyone else feel a pressure in their chest?" No one responded. "I mean at least you were found in a shell–"

"A turtle shell," Mary interjected. "By the road–"started Texas

"It was the shore of the lake or stream, I forget." Mary interjected again.

"It could have been worse," Fred slid into a seat at the end of the table and poured a mug of tea for himself. "So, you're not going to take the summer position? You're going to stay here with us?" He said, squeezing the mug as if he were to wring juice from it.

Mary took a long sip. "It doesn't matter where or how I found you or what the day is called. What matters is that you are mine to love and care for, and however it happened, I will always do that for you. Now, Texas, you're eighteen and you're done with school, the world's different now. I think you're right not to take that summer internship. It's not going to be easy, and, you'd have to move to a large place, and the people, oh, the many people." Mary shook her head. "Stay here."

It was comfortable. It was what she knew. "Yeah, I think I'll stay here. There is nothing I really want." Texas laughed in her tea a little.

"That's great! You know yourself. Nothing is sometimes the hardest thing to have. But, like I said, you're eighteen and we should have the sex talk again."

Texas spat the tea back in her cup and decided against it, taking an even longer drought of her tea and sat up straight. "This is good," she sarcastically intoned and looked up, making the mistake of–

Gabby locked eyes with her, and for a moment, she shivered as her stomach tightened. There was a burning in her pocket, and she knew she had to do something. The breath wouldn't come; a memory not in view was pushing its way forward. She clenched her teeth as her abdominal muscles flexed involuntarily. Gabby took a breath. "I brought it with me," herm said, pointing to the tea. Texas looked down at it. "You know, there used to be wars over tea. Sometimes it was the only source of nutrients for people. I'm glad you like it. This one is strong and powerful." He finally looked away and down at his trumpet. "This thing worked when I left home with it."

Mary was eating her breakfast, and Fred had his face turned to a book when Texas bent over, grabbing the table. Bile was in the back of her throat; an acidic tinge ate away at the walls of her esophagus.

"Oh, so you have a home?" Fred said, keeping his eyes down. "As in you're not homeless?"

"That doesn't matter. Herm said herm needed a place to stay. I took a vow long ago, and while I may not wear the habit anymore, I still hold true to–" Mary said, making the sign of the cross.

"I wouldn't call it a home, as much as a place I live. But it's nice there. I thought I would travel for a bit and see the world." Gabby smiled at Texas, who was mouthing words without a sound, her eyes bulging, and the lump in her throat that was clawing its way out of her moved to the back of her mouth. She remembered last night, parts of it. The key came out of her.

"And the trumpet?" Fred added.

Texas looked over, pleading with trembling eyes, her hand in the air ready to slam it down, forcing them to take notice as Gabby, with herm unblinking eyes fixed on hers. "Do you have something to show us?" Herm asked. "There is something you need to let out, something to share. Are you still hiding it? "Gabby said in a whisper. Instinctually, with Texas's other hand, she pulled the key from her pocket and ran it through her fingers. Her heart slowed in beats, and her muscles relaxed.

Texas took a deep gasp of air, sharply pulling the attention of her family. "Texas, no need to act out." Mary said.

Texas panted and looked at each of them. Fred looked up and stared for a bit. "Did you swallow down the wrong pipe?" He spoke.

"No, I just felt a weight on me." Texas regained her steady breath and sat back down. "On, what dear? You shouldn't eat so fast." Mary said, keeping her eye on the next round of eggs.

Gabby looked at the key. "You shouldn't hide such things. They are precious." Texas looked down and ran the metallic object around her fingers. It was just a key. "Where did you get that?" Mary added, taking the empty plate of food from Fred.

Texas pulled back, "I threw it up."

"Why would you eat a key?" Fred asked matter-a-factly.

Gabby leaned over and reached out to grab the key from Texas's hand. She pulled back and clenched it tight.

"Of course it's yours, it is just amazing you had one. You should keep it close at all times; don't let anyone touch it. They are rarer than most would think." Gabby said, now keeping his attention on the key. "This was a wonderful day, friends, thank you for counting me among your kind. A key, a trumpet, wow! It's like the world's going to end. And here we are."

"Oh, that's lovely." Mary said, smiling at him. She gently grabbed the key from Texas, "this is very pretty, I have an idea."

"Mom!" Texas exclaimed.

Mary took the key to a sideboard and opened up a drawer that had various knick-knacks. Pulling an old, thin leather rope from the drawer and looping it through the end, she made a small necklace and placed it around Texas's head. "There you go. Very suiting." She said, smiling at her.

"More tea, friend?" Gabby asked Texas. "We are not friends." Texas stated flatly.

"Oh, right, I'm sorry." The angel stood up and bowed. "My name is Gabby, and I am a friend to your mother. Now, I am a friend to you." Herm extended herm's hand to shake. "We didn't shake before; we should shake now to officially be friends."

"Now, not that kind of friend," Mary started. "See, this is why we need to have the sex talk. You could have been confused. There are friends and there are friends. He is a friend, in that, he is nice, and I said herm could sleep on the couch. While we are on the topic of sex, the pen–"

"Thank you!" Fred and Texas said in unison.

Texas stuffed the key into her shirt. Gabby looked at it one last time. "What a glorious day!" He said as he took a deep breath and blew his trumpet.

"Why are you blowing your trumpet anyway?" Texas asked.

"Because I'm heralding the world's end, I thought I told you this." Gabby said quietly, grinning like a fool.

"It can't come soon enough," she said, stuffing the last fork full of eggs in her mouth.

The Second Bit

"Only dull people quote others."

[August B. Summers]

Her bike clicked as the chain bounced against the frame, her dark coat flapped in a light breeze, and for a moment she thought she could make it through town without–

"Slow down!" A bulbous man with a squeaky voice shouted. Sheriff Plain was wagging his finger as Texas rode by him, her hand tight against the handlebars, her middle finger down and out of sight as her back faced his glare. She continued past Fred's parents' coffee bar and through the main street shops, where Mrs. Mpta brushed away the last leaves that dotted Main Street.

The sidewalks ended, and the houses gave way to trees before hitting the only stop sign out of the town and into the back roads. She biked up and down hills and past the remnants of Mr. Bacon's homestead's foundation and stopped at the low, crumbling stone wall that encircled the old town. It was guarded by the final sign people read before departing; Now leaving Nowhere, North Dakota, We Will Miss You!

She made a sharp turn on a quaint, long, desolate road that came out directly after the sign and down its winding path into a sun-filled field and open grove where a small stone mansion stood. The paved roadway gave way to loose stone up to an eight-foot door adorned with two pillars wrapped in stone holly, the left one slightly smaller than the right.

Texas rolled around to the back, jumped off her bike and into the servant's door, turned off the alarm, looked around at the gilded walls with cracks beginning to appear in the corners. With one deep breath, she grabbed the scrubs from the servant's closet and went to work scrubbing the upstairs bathroom, working the cleaner, then on to the tub, the marble walls, and putting on the special gloves for the toilet - her favorite part. After the cleaning, she would watch it flush and, for a moment, absorbed herself in the swirling; always to the left, her eyes following a single crest that ebbed and flowed, surfing along the bowl.

Downstairs was a king. A tall, pale king named Pindar. Well, not a real king, though he had land, title (esq., dr., or something like that), and a small army to his name, he couldn't count himself among the aristocracy as he inherited nothing but work. He was just that, to make things work. Like a tinkerer or engineer, he would put duct tape on this and that and, in doing so, would make money and ensure his power.

At this moment, he was lost in what was a strange dream. What was odd about it was that he was awake while it was happening. As if a memory dangled upon a silver thread bouncing before his eyes, he remembered a machine, enormous in its construction, as if one had put half the heavens in mechanical form. It was veiled, alive, and as if repeating in both color and number, but there it affected the senses. It affected the touch and the sight and the feel and smell-

He was back; it was a darkened, acid smell that danced around his nose now. A clear odor of his coffee, which seemed to be cold. He heard the toilet flush and followed the sound as his flannel shirt and pants scratched against his skin.

"What an odd thing to look at," the tall, thin man said, watching Texas from the door. "Mr. Pindar. I get lost in the swirl, I guess." Texas said, she stood up straight and pushed

her red hair to the front of her face.

"How odd–"he stopped and looked into the bowl, "Yes, I see it now. The Fibonacci sequence, almost swarm theory in motion, before muttering to himself 1.6180..." And he trailed off, glaring at the key around her neck. "Is that yours?" He asked, moving slightly forward.

"I don't know. Wait, what?" Texas winced, grasping the key, trying to hide it once again within the confines of her shirt.

He moved his needle finger out and behind the key, hooking it and bringing it close to his face before she could take it away. "This. I feel as if it's for me. Do you know what this is?"

"That's an odd phrase," she replied, stuck on the middle statement. She squeezed her sweaty palms and instantly straightened, her mind flittered between bugs and bees, as she mimicked Mr. Pindar's high tone. She stopped and clasped her lips tight, biting them shut from the inside.

"Is it?" He moved his hand away, not noting the tone. "It's meaningful." And he moved further away. "I'm going to have to tell someone about that."

"It's nothing." Texas said.

"Then why wear it? Where did it come from?"

"I, well, you won't believe it." She recalculated. "I mean it's weird." More specifically. "I dreamed I threw it up last night. I don't really know but I found it next to me, or I guess I had swallowed it or something, I don't know."

The man walked to the next room, which was his closet. Texas put her eyes to the ground and retreated further into the bathroom. She had seen this movie: The rich man, the young woman... But he pulled out a suit, put it on piece by piece. Texas continued, staving off the cheap plot line that she was beginning to play out. "Have you used it yet?" He said.

"Used it?"

He finished with a sharp coat that hugged his chest. "Yes. It is a key. It should unlock something."

"I don't know where is goes." Texas said.

"I don't think most do." Pinder said, walking in the frame of Texas again, "My dear. I have to leave now, and I will be back in seven hours. I'm going to need you to work on getting this house into shape. I will be back with a friend. You will be here... with your key."

Texas breathed out and relaxed as Pindar walked from the room. "You know, sir, I wanted to talk to you." Texas said.

Pindar stopped in the hall and was bouncing his fingers across his thumb and making notes in the air around him as his eyes bounced from one imaginary idea to the next.

"Well, I got that internship with your company, but I don't know..."

"I have need of you. We have to make you useful. Oh, and my friend is not a friend, but he is odd. I have to make this clear. Don't use the key." Pindar's eyes were moving back and forth as his breathing became more erratic. "I repeat. Don't use the key."

"Okay... sir..."

Pindar stopped and looked out of the window, pressing his thumb to the tips of his fingers, counting in his head. "Do you like money?"

"Yes?" Her inflection involuntarily ticked up. The cheap movie played again. She clenched her fist and held her breath.

"Why?" He turned to her again, looking at the key.

"I..." Texas flushed red and cracked her knuckles, wide-eyed, "Well..."

"We will arrive, you will be here, please bring donuts." He paused to straighten his coat, finishing, "It is important that you don't use that key."

Quit, she said in her head. This time, her eyes met his, and she didn't blink.

"Men in my position are used to this arrangement. We ask for things, and people give them. But it's always about discretion. Mm," Pindar said as if deep in thought. "Keep the house nice." From the hall, Mr. Pindar smiled awkwardly and made his way out of the room, whispering "998749...".

She smiled because, what else could she do, and she assumed it was expected of her; she retreated back to the bathroom and flushed the toilet again, watching the water swirl once more around the bowl to get her head clean before~ "Have to wash away the rest of the soap." Texas said to keep her mind on her task.

She calmed. By the time she was downstairs to tackle the kitchen, Mr. Pindar's car was at the house, and with a thud, the front door shut, the alarm beeped, and she knew he had forgotten she was still in the house. Shoes off and a cheese plate full of things he didn't eat but for some reason kept around "in case," which she figured meant: In case she was hungry. She walked through the gallery that was his home, noting the things of value.

By midafternoon, Texas was back on the road, biking towards the center of town, debating whether to go back or not. She sped down to the place where Fred spent his days cleaning and sweeping the floors at his parents' coffee shop – The Shaky Hands. This time, he was reading a book on business aptly named The Business of Piracy that had a man with a dollar sign hook on his right hand. His mother was hanging up another cross on the wall to make a total of 42. His father was delivering two cups of his finest roasted espresso in blue and silver demitasses to a couple on the other side of the room.

It was too crowded today, an older man reading a dampened, tattered parchment sat near the counter, while a couple, at least that is what their feet told us, smiled awkwardly at one another. And a woman with two 5-gallon gas cans and a packet of matches, about ready to order coffee.

Texas sauntered to the counter next to Fred and took a sip from his cup.

"What are you reading?" Texas snooped, peering over his shoulder, half a hair from his ear. He couldn't hide the smile or the flushed cheeks.

He put his book away and pushed her face from him. "You back from work?"

"Yeah." She fingered the key under her shirt.

Fred looked like he was going to reach for her hand, and she pulled back. "Did you really throw that up?"

"Yes. Why do you doubt me?" Texas bristled. "No, it's just weird, right?"

"Mr. Pindar was interested in it. He said, 'Don't use it.'" She imitated his high voice. "I need to find out what this is for. I need your help."

"Really?" Fred leaned in. "So, am I going to meet Mr. Pindar? Were you serious about staying here? A.T.L.A.S. industries is a big deal, and I guarantee Mr. Pindar could get you anything at the company."

"I don't want to work there, or really anywhere. It's comfortable here. Focus on the key." Texas mimicked Mr. Pindar again.

"That's what I'm talking about!" Fred exclaimed, "You have something of value to them.

The biggest company in the world, the man behind it is interested in that thing you threw up." Texas rolled her eyes. "What you said this morning, if you're comfortable here, I'm sure my parents could hire you on, but let's see what he is willing to pay for that key. Think about it, this could set us up for life." Fred finished.

Texas drifted in and out, thinking about the key and the coffee shop and the key and Mary and the key and home and the key and Mary and the coffee shop. "I don't really want to work at the coffee shop either. I don't really want to do anything, Fred."

"That's what I'm talking about!" Fred grabbed her shoulders.

"Well, maybe you should pray on it, because you're going to need a miracle." Fred's mother interjected, bringing over a plate of fufu and two coffees. "You both just need to pray and work." She said, shaking her finger at them.

"Thanks, mom." Fred said. They both stared at her until she said "mhm." And left. "He's going to give you like a thousand dollars, I mean ten thousand. That's the cost of a dinner for him. He's going to give you a lot. What would you do if you could do anything?" "You can't ask questions like that."

"Come on, play along. What would you do if you could do anything?"

"I would do nothing. You know, my mom says nothing is the hardest thing to do."

"And how would you do that?"

"I don't know. Maybe that is a prayer. Like a genie God, right? I pray, and I get whatever I want. I don't know." She said. Then she turned her head and noted a cross at the register. "Why is your mom hanging up another cross? "

"Don't hide from the money questions. How much money do you think you'd need, and that's how much you should ask. I'll negotiate!" Fred instinctively reached out and grabbed her hand.

Texas pulled back. Conversation over.

Fred started again. "A prayer. Right? Like if I prayed for something, I'm wishing for it.

I don't know. Maybe I'll wish, and he's just going to pay. I wish I could work for A.T.L.A.S. Industries." Fred ventured. "And then I'd make enough that you wouldn't have to work... if we were together or something..."

Texas was staring at the cross that Fred's mother was hanging. It was a thin cross made of palm leaves, folded and glued down. "Like you want to be a pirate," Texas began.

"Business owner." Fred corrected her.

She pulled out the key, and from down the counter, a spit-take happened. An older man bowed over, chattering his wooden teeth. A single finger sticking out. "Let me see that!" He gruffly said, pointing at the key.

Fred stood up, placing himself between the oncoming geriatric and Texas. She pushed Fred aside. "No." she firmly said.

The old man stopped. "It looks like mine." He said, peering down at her from behind his nose. He put on a pair of spectacles. "Hmmm, yes. Just like mine."

Texas looked at Fred and took the necklace off with the key. "What do you mean, it looks like yours?"

"You threw that up?" He said as if Texas had somehow wronged him. Texas looked at Fred again, paler than usual.

"Yep. I had the same look. Ben found me after I threw up. Have you used it yet?" the old man asked.

"Ben?"

"Yeah, a friend I had. Look, that key is nothing but trouble." He waved his hand in dismissal.

"What does it do?" Texas asked. "I don't know?"

"What do you mean, 'you don't know?'" It has to open or turn on something." Fred entered the conversation.

"Yeah, it does something like that. But be careful, a lot of people want that because they can't make one of their own." The man said. "I see you don't care. You don't have a care in the world." He paused. "Well, Good luck," he said, walking out.

"No, wait..." Fred exclaimed, reaching out after him.

"Nope, I have things to do now." The man chattered his wooden teeth.

"But..." and the thunderous sound of a horn blared through the sky and rocketed and shook the ground they stood on. Texas grabbed Fred to steady herself. He smiled and grabbed her hand.

We're out of bits

"Dark is the deep and deep is the dark,
but when you find a spot, you recognize the spot is all."

[The guys down the road]

Within a mile of Shaky Hands, Gabby slowly sauntered down the pavement and into town, making herm way to the center where a small park sat, complete with a gazebo tucked between two trees.

Herm sat in full lotus directly center between the crisscross of boards, fingering herm's horn, trying to blow through the mouthpiece, but only getting sputters. Herm waited. One by one, the townspeople came out to look. Mrs. Mpta, who feared herm might track leaves onto her clear sideways. Then Mr. Flapp stopped walking his dogs, and then Sheriff Plain stopped to watch with the small crowd.

"Well, do something!" Mrs. Mpta said to the Sheriff.

"She's not breaking any laws, per se. I mean, not right now." The Sheriff turned his head to the sky. "I mean, not any real laws." The crowd grew.

"What of Public Spectacle?" Mr. Flapp asked. "Made up." The Sheriff explained.

"And being rude on a Thursday," a tiny man in back yelled

"Also made up. They are just rules we all agreed to." The Sheriff pulled out his little book of ordinances. "Let's see if there aren't any real laws she is breaking. Public indecency?" He looked at herm. "Well, her legs are crossed while she is wearing a dress."

"Everyone, take a step back to see if we can see her whoohay!" Mrs. Mpta said. And everyone stepped back and looked under herm's dress. Gabby opened one eye and pulled up herm dress slightly to reveal a small set of shorts.

"What about being ugly?" A woman asked.

The Sheriff flipped through his book. "Nope, not seeing anything in here about that. And I don't think she would have fit under a law such as that; we would need an objective opinion on ugly." Everyone looked at one another, "Yeah, I don't see any way to qualify that one."

Jorge was jogging. He was new to the town, having just moved there from a major metropolis. He had purchased one of the small residences up on the hill, where all the new people in town had to purchase due to some unknown law. He was a retired, in his mid-thirties, and wanted for

nothing save for some peace and a good public spectacle; and that is when he saw the crowd and the woman (herm) on the knoll in the gazebo. Talking to no one in particular, he elbowed his way in and started, "Oh, would you look at that." He said, walking up. "I bet she is looking to spread her religion, at least she is going about it in a good way. I went to New York City once, and there was a man who was looking like he had lost everything and was still wandering, and there he was with a T-shirt saying Read that bible. And I was like, it looks like the bible brought him there. I mean, if you are going to tell someone to read the bible, at least make yourself look presentable, so people say, 'yeah!' I want to join that religion. Not, oh god, if I join that religion, I have to sit with him..."

And everyone looked at Jorge.

The Sheriff slapped him. "Not in my town. People are allowed to believe whatever they want, but not that! Sitting like she's better than everyone else. Look at her, quietly contemplating, not bothering anyone about her purpose in life. It's unnatural, I tell you."

Everyone shook their heads in agreement. Mrs. Mpta walked up to Jorge and slapped him. "It's nice to see the newer members of this community getting involved."

"Why did you slap me?" Jorge asked. "Speak when spoken to." She said.

Mr. Flapp slapped Jorge. "Thank you for your input. I'm glad we don't have that ugly law."

"Thank you?" Jorge said.

"Now--" The Sheriff pulled up his belt to begin, but--

"Wait!" A voice shouted. It was Gabby, herm trumpet at herm side. Everyone clasped their chest and bent a little in with their knees; some grabbed their heads at the pressure, like being pulled under water, and slowly twisted around the crowd. Herm put the trumpet to herm lips and took a breath.

"Oh, not this again." Someone sounding much like Texas barked a moment before a deafening trumpet sound was heard across the sky, atonal, and a hint of red oak found its way to the back of everyone's throat, accompanied by bile and the morning breakfast. Plain looked behind him and made contact with Texas, her face squinted up and her tongue pressing against the roof of her mouth.

"You know him?" The Sheriff tried to ask Texas; she walked her bike up the grassy hill, shaking her head.

"Sadly." She said.

Stuffing his previous meal back into his stomach with a hard swallow, the Sheriff stood up straight, "Then you go over there and tell her... him to be normal! Go sweep up leaves like Mrs. Mpta or build small miniatures of nature in the basement like Mr. Flapp or conduct backyard plays with woodland creatures-- I don't care, just make sure she is quiet."

Texas walked up to Gabby as herm was taking an impossibly long and deep breath. "Stop!" She said reaching out to herm.

"Texas, friend! How are you? It is good to see you again." Herm said, focusing herm unblinking eyes on Texas.

"What are you doing here? Why aren't you with my mother?" "Haven't you seen?" Herm smiled unblinkingly at Texas. "Seen what?"

Gabby pointed at the crowd. "Excuse me, do you know where the house at the end of town is?" A voice said. Texas felt pulled by an inexplicable force, as if an inkling, somewhere deep in her, was pushing her to go forward. It was like an impulse, a direction, so sure and purposeful yet hers from within. "Why aren't you following her?" Gabby asked Texas. The woman in the crowd's voice interjected. "Excuse me, I'm looking for the house at the end of the town." The crowd parted, and through it came a woman, eighteen or so, blonde with a grey hue. "Excuse me," she said, asking indiscriminately. "I'm looking for the house at the end of the town. Any idea where it is?"

She turned to see Texas and walked right up to her, "Excuse me," she said. Texas looked down at her hands that were clenching two full five-gallon jugs of gasoline and a pack of matches in one hand. "I'm looking for the house at the end of the town."

"I don't know that place," Texas said.

"Okay," she said and turned to ask no one in particular again.

"Ask her about the gas cans." Herm piped in; herm's voice curled over Texas's shoulder. "Wait, I need to know why you are holding the gas cans," Texas said.

"I'm going to burn down the house at the end of the town." She plainly said. Texas's eyes darted to Sheriff Plain, directing people away from Gabby.

"You shouldn't say that." Texas motioned with her hand, pointing at the Sheriff. "Why, it's true." And she turned to the Sheriff, "Excuse me, do you know where the house at the end of the town is?"

Sheriff Plain looked at her. "Why are you asking?" "Because I'm going to burn it down."

Plain gave a thoughtful nod. Texas tensed and blurted out. "I'm sure she doesn't mean it."

"Oh, no. I mean it. I'm going to burn it down to the ground." The woman repeated. Plain looks at Texas and back at the woman. "Don't know that house." He said. "Would you like to help me burn it down?"

"You can't say that!" Texas knew better. She shouldn't be involved. Then you're responsible.

"Why not?" The strange woman asked again.

"Because he's the Sheriff." Texas motioned to Plain, who was clearly busy ushering the town's people away.

Plain looked at them. "She can burn it down, she's looking for the house outside of the town, I'm only concerned with what's in town. And there are no laws about carrying around gas; if there were, I'd have to arrest every car. Wouldn't work."

Gabby blew the horn again, but only a pale A came forth. The woman looked over at herm. "What's his deal?" she asked Texas.

"I'm signaling the end of the world," Gabby said, and herm blew again, nothing but squeaks came out. "Don't worry, I'll get it soon!" Gabby said with a smile

We're on to 'things

"This is my nutshell"

[Teddy the Bear]

Later.

Without fail, on the second street aptly named, 2nd Rd, Gabby was walking up and down polishing herm horn, trying to get it to work while closely being followed by Sheriff Plain at the urging of the men and women who quietly looked out of their front window.

The Sheriff was flipping through a book of ordinances, trying to keep pace. "Now, I realize it says, if the horn is to signal the end of the world, then the noise ordinances do not apply to said player. But I don't think that is what the founding fathers had in mind. You see, they were a religious community, strange in their liking and kicked out of most towns for their beliefs, but I don't think they thought the end would ever come, and that is why they put it in the ordinances. I don't want to, but I will, I will ask Judge Henry George to get an injunction." Sheriff Plain said.

Gabby stopped. "Now, under the city charter set up by Amen, it clearly states~"

"I know what it states, I just read it to you... How do I know the end is even near, let alone that you are heralding it?" He said.

Gabby stopped for a moment and thought. "Faith, I guess. I mean, look at the sky, it's blue."

"The sky is always blue."

"Ah yes, but now it is a blue blue. You see a sure sign the end is near." Gabby continued down the road.

"Now, look here! There is fine print. It states that the instrument will be for the good of all those who listen."

"And it is! Listen, it's the end of the world!" Gabby took a deep breath. There was a small cat-like noise as if it were wrung clean in a washer. "Nope, that is still out of tune."

"Sir, ma'am, did you say your name was Gabby? That would probably be easier." Sheriff Plain ran in front of Gabby, puffed out his chest.

"Yes, well, no. I mean, my name is Gabriel, but you can call me Gabby."

Sheriff Plain took out his pad and started writing everything down. "And are you a Mr.?"

"No, it's Herm. Herm Gabby."

"Herm? Yes, I'm not a him or a her, I don't have a gender, I just exist. That's it. Here, so we can forgo the questions, let me show you..." Herm started to pull up herm's robe.

"No, that is okay, thank you, and you are..." The Sheriff continued. "What are you writing down."

"I'm going to write you a citation."

"A citation, amazing! What is it?" Gabby clenched his fists, shaking them excitedly, smiling like a fool.

"It's a ticket. I figure this will stop you for now, and we can figure out if it's legal later." Sheriff Plain ripped off the sheet and handed it to Gabby.

"That's fine, but I won't pay it. As I stated, your town founder said I–"

"First, he said it was for townspeople, but you are not. Second, he said it was for instruments that were working well. And I don't know it's the end of the world."

"But I'm telling you-"

"Right, but you don't have the authority."

"I have the authority of God. Well, I used to... haven't seen herm in a while."

But Sheriff Plain was looking away to see a man with a white streak through his hair dressed in a white tunic and full armor, trailed by a younger man who was struggling to carry an enormous sword, going from door to door. Behind them was a character dressed in black, shaded as if the sun was out of reach, carrying a map and a scythe. Plain dropped the citation and turned to confront the new stranger. Gabby looked over and gasped–

Mary took another sip of tea and stood to answer the knocking at the door, "Gabby, I found some Chapstick for your lips. I bet they are blistered by..." She opened the door and saw Gabby crying.

"What's wrong, dear. Come in, can I make you something?" "Saw someone in town and I feared they were here for you." "Who was it?"

"Oh, let's not bother with it." Herm pushed past her and sat at the table, brewing another pot of tea. "Here drink up, tea is good for you. It will help." Herm rushed through, extending the steaming mug. "I love you, Mary. You are a good woman. Come, where is your favorite place to be in the house?"

"Well, thank you." She walked into the other room and sat in a pink-laced, high-back chair with soft crushed velvet covering its curves.

"Drink up." Gabby said, tipping the mug toward her lips. "Oh, I feel dizzy." She grabbed the chair arm and sat down. "Yeah, I figured."

"I don't think...."

"No, you don't have to anymore."

And with that, Mary transpired from this world, and her body lay limp. Gabby kissed her forehead and let a tear fall from herm eye.

Outside of Shaky Hands, Texas, hopped on her bike, "I have to get back to work. Fred, I think I got this weird thing with Mr. Pindar, but in case I need it." Her voice modulated a bit, "I want you out front, you know, in case things go wrong." She stood up straight. "I can handle it, of course, but if I can't and if I run out or you hear me scream, I need you to, like, run there," butter him up, Texas thought, "be the big, strong, sacrificial..."

A gray-haired man put his hand through his hair and then opened the door to The Shaky Hands Coffee House at the corner of Main and 3rd, Nowhere, North Dakota; he entered, trailed by a young man perspiring and biceps bulging from a long sword in his arms and armor slung across his back that caught only the eye of Texas. The young man took the sword and armor and laid them next to the table neatly on the floor with reverence. "Bob," The old man said as he took a seat. "Don't forget to make the sign of the cross."

They were both garbed in priests' robes with wooden rosaries around their necks and were but sinew and muscle from their long journey. Thomas, the older of the two, took out a flask and sniffed it before a small nip that gave him a bit of warmth. Bob, the younger of the two, leaned back and stretched, hearing his back groan.

Bob shook his head in agreement. "Yes, Father Thomas. Your armor is safe."

Texas looked at Fred before Fred said, "I'll protect you. I have a sword, or something, too." Patting his side, but only finding a pen.

Still on point. "Don't show up with me, though. Wait thirty minutes after I leave to get there." Texas said as she gathered her things and caught eyes with the strapping men, donned in their religious accouterments. Texas left, taking time to glance at them before-

"Would you like a nip?" Thomas asked, holding out a flask as he watched the redhead take off on her bike.

"No, I'm okay." Bob said. It was quite the day for sitting quietly, unlike playing solitaire, where the more you want to play by yourself, the more people want to be near you; here, people move away, akin to a week-old cheese.

"Why are we here?" Bob began.

"I don't know." Thomas said. "Let's ask." He held up his finger, and Mrs. Mpta quietly walked over from behind the counter.

"Hello, welcome to Shaky Hands Coffery. Would you like to order akara or chin chin?" She said.

He ignored her question. "Hello, I am Thomas of the Inquisition. This is Bob, a fellow knight, and we are on a quest. Do you know why we are here?"

She looked them up and down. "No."

Bob straightened up and repeated, "Do you know why you are here?" He said to Mrs.Mpta.

"Because I own this. I like making coffee... speaking of, what would you like to order?"

She looked at the flask. "I'll brew you up a nice dark roast; it goes with anything."

"That would be good. Thank you." Thomas said. He turned his attention to Bob, "Bob, we've been asking people all day why we are here, and no one has an answer."

Bob shook his head in agreement. He was rehearsing in his head. Just the right words... There was a long pause, and Bob looked up, taking a deep breath. "I think it is time we parted ways. I feel like I must go west, and if no one can tell us why we are here, then maybe it's time for me to find out why I'm here."

Thomas shook his head up and down in agreement. “I am here. And until I am told otherwise, I’m going to stay. It was good to travel with you; I hope our paths cross again.” Thomas took another nip.

Their chests grew heavy, and for a moment, Thomas’s face grew pale and gaunt, his heart pounding in his ears as Bob’s mouth shriveled and dried. They looked out of the window, across the road to see a man, maybe a man, walking slowly across the street.

“Oh, no.” Thomas said.

“Do you feel something upon your chest?” Bob asked, but Thomas was already up and running outside to herm. Bob quickly joined.

“I know you.” Thomas said, running across the road to block Gabby’s path. “You’re... you’re an angel!”

Robert ran outside carrying the sword, ready to unsheathe. Thomas turned to the other priest, “Don’t engage with it! Everyone is so impressed by an angel. They are terrible. Just the worst.” He then turned to the angel and pleaded. “Do you know why we are here?”

“I lost a friend, please leave me alone.” Gabby said Head down.

“You lost a friend? Perhaps we can find them for you? We need something to do.” Gabby shook his head back and forth.

Thomas stopped. “Dead? But you’re an angel, and if your friend was with you, surely they are in heaven, is that reason to celebrate, not mourn? You of all creatures should know this.”

“You don’t understand, I don’t mourn for them, I mourn for those that were left behind.”

Robert made the sign of the cross, and Thomas folded his hands in prayer. “I am sorry. What was your friend’s name?” Thomas asked.

“Mary Rhodes.” Gabby said, herm’s voice sounded as if a thousand were speaking as one. “Mary Rhodes?” Thomas turned to Bob and exclaimed. “That’s why!”

“Please, now I must mourn.” And with that, Gabby spread herm wings and let herm light shine upon all as the sounds of children singing echoed from the sky, Bob dropped to his knees from the pressure and wept without knowing. Mrs.

Mpta walked outside, bending slightly from the last weight of the angel's presence. She took a deep breath and calmly said, "You forgot your coffee."

Thomas grabbed both mugs. "Thank you," while Bob tried to lift himself as water dripped from his nose. "Do you have any sugar?"

"I'll be right back with some for you." Mrs. Mpta said, turning slowly, as a wave of sadness settled on her shoulders.

Thomas took a sip, "They will do that. You feel what they are feeling. Angels, always showing off."

THERE ARE A NUMBER OF THINGS...

"That's not possible."

[A Doctor outside of July 15,1997,
Podiatry Conference, New York, New York]

Later.

Charles Pindar, the lanky man, stark and austere, who liked numbers, stood waiting for Texas. He was rolling over the number 131 in his head, liked the way it tasted and smelled, its crisp tone, he wished it were on a page as it accentuated how it would feel between his fingers. Numbers were best when they were on the page; screens couldn't give you the same tactile sensation. He was having dreams again. Dreams while he was awake again. He was working with people; there was a tower that pierced the clouds and led to an orb that circled the globe.

3. There were three. The number three came to his head; he could see the beauty in it. It had a pale blue to it. A kind, simple number, not like pie, of course, the most beautiful of them all, like light dancing on the water, something brilliant, kind, and warm. Third rock. Three fingers. Third left. Third.... He looked at his paper and saw the number 70491, and it made his face red. He closed his eyes and took a breath.

3.141592... yes.

He looked out the windows on the flat landscape that was North Dakota, waiting for a moment to race across his hundred thousand-acre woods. Maybe today was the day he would quit and do something with his numbers. His guest was downstairs at the front door, and he could hear Texas let herself in.

As he descended the ornate oak staircase, looking for Texas, and was going to ask her not to be seen, when an olive-skinned man, caked in what looked like pearls that were slowly beginning to crack under the power of thought, sinew, and muscle came through the door behind her.

"This is an odd home; the ceiling doesn't have good proportions, it looks misshapen.

Angular" were his first words. "But it works."

"It's the new style." Pindar answered.

The man walked in, owning the place with arms wide and grand gestures. He gave Pindar a hug and whispered in his ear. "Where is she?"

Pinder cleared his throat and led the man around the house looking for her until they arrived at the main living room, where Texas was staring at an oil painting of a woman dancing upon Greek ruins that-. "Texas, that is your name, right? I sometimes forget." She was interrupted. "It's the 16th century. Started the Renaissance. When the great year turned." Pindar said, then whispered 3, 5, 7, 11, 13... "This is my..."

"I'm Atlas!" The man shouted and rapidly advanced, embracing her. He smelled like oak, his arms were gentle though, encompassing her with each finger pressing against her. He pulled back and looked at her chest.

"Pindar! You look good, you didn't touch the key, did you?" Atlas said. Texas felt her body crumple as his hand pressed against her. She should run.

"Only slightly."

"Hmmm, okay. But a key holder should be treated better than that." His eyes moved to her and locked. Texas stiffened and looked for the exits. "Come, we shall feast!" He looked down at her and ran his fingers along her arms. "Look at me. You are very special." He wrapped his arm around her and led her forward as a doll to the kitchen.

There was a pot of lentil soup on the stove, but Texas didn't know how it got there. Pindar scooped out a bowl for Atlas, "Lentil soup?"

"I'm okay..." She said, and Atlas walked her to the table and placed her in a seat at the roundest area in the kitchen. "I thought you said we were having a feast?" Texas asked. She forgot the doughnuts.

Atlas sat across from her, slowly eating a bowl of lentils that was placed before him. "We are. This is a feast." His eyes didn't leave her; they lingered, and while she could have sworn he was eating, she heard the spoon ting against the bowl, the soup drip, and a slurp. She didn't see his mouth move. It was locked in position as an endless squint as if a pain was echoing across his mind as he fixated on the key. Her heart inched its way up, pressing against her ribs and choking her ears. She leaned forward and–

"I forgot the doughnuts." She said. No one answered.

Finally, "I know you're thinking roasts and pheasants...." He sipped some more. The spell broke. The soup looks as you would expect. Her ears relaxed and she took a breath "But, I don't eat meat. It's not responsible, and this right here is all anyone ever needs." Atlas explained. "So, what is your purpose in this world?"

Texas looked at the two men and paused." I don't know. Mr. Pindar said you wanted the key." Pausing. "And, doughnuts, which I forgot." She started taking the key out.

"Don't worry about the doughnuts! Where are you going in this life?" Atlas asked. He sat back; his smile put her at ease. "We want to help you know."

Showing her actions with her hands. "I'm not going anywhere," Texas responded. "That's a shame, all people should be going somewhere." Atlas said.

And Texas looked around for an easy escape. Thinking, asking, this is what everyone does in every conversation. They couldn't just sit and enjoy silence.

"If you're not going anywhere, what are you going to do with that key? You see, I need that key; it can make dreams come true, and my dream is-"

The house alarm stopped them.

Outside was a woman. Actually, it was the women, both gas cans empty, with the fuel sprayed across the wooden entrance, set ablaze, fire dancing in her eyes.

Pindar looked at her unperturbed, muttering something to himself. Atlas came out, assessed the situation, and walked back in.

"What are you doing!?" Texas ran out and demanded. She watched the stone pillars turn black and the ebb and flow of the red and yellow crested upon the wood slats. She stood up straight, smiling, and put her blond hair in a bun. Her lithe figure was swaying back and forth as she was muttering something under her breath. Then she looked at Texas.

"I found the house at the edge of town." She said, watching the house slowly be engulfed.

Atlas emerged from the front door with what looked like a battle axe and sword. "This crime demands a painful end!" He roared.

Texas froze.

Atlas bounded toward the woman, and with each step, he swung his weapon wildly. The woman darted backward and moved faster than Texas could register.

The woman and Atlas danced as swans in a choreographed play, wings slicing through the air. Where he lunged, she parried, and where she ran, he met her in a tornado's embrace.

The woman eventually made her way back to Texas. "Come on." She said, grinning like a fool, and grasped Texas by the wrist. "This is going to be grand!" She exclaimed.

Atlas leaned forward and darted to Texas, his sword pointing forward, tip driving at her head, but the woman pulled on Texas's arm and yanked her from the scene. Before Texas registered, her feet were moving; the two women were at full sprints with Atlas in pursuit.

Within a second, he was on them, swinging his sword, nearly taking off Texas's head. "Key holder!" Atlas screamed and stopped, realizing he had almost hit her. After a pause, he resumed his chase. The woman, laughing, was faster than she looked and four feet ahead of Texas, looking back every once in a while. "Come on!" she yelled as Texas felt a hand grab the wisps of stray hair, plucking out two strands. They made it to the end of the driveway and turned toward town. Atlas was pacing next to Texas and raised his axe above his head. "I'm not after you," Atlas assured her before releasing the ax that flew forward and glided an inch past the woman's head.

The wall to town was fast approaching, as was a car that had an ax buried in the front grill. It stopped, and Sheriff Plain got out right before the wall. Texas and the girl crossed the town threshold, and Atlas stopped. Everyone looked at the line of town. Atlas put his sword down and crossed the line. "Officer," he said.

"Inside these walls is my jurisdiction." Plain said to Atlas.

"I know how the world works. I own it." Atlas said.

The Sheriff looked at Atlas and the ax. "I know. And I'll let this go this once."

Atlas nodded, then began. "Texas, I would still like to offer you something for your key."

"Leave us alone!" Texas said scream.

"Done. Give me the key." Atlas said, holding out his hand.

Fred rode up on his bike. "Texas!" He said, looking at the axe hilt sticking out of Sheriff Plain's car.

Texas pulled it out from around her neck and became shaky. Her hand twitched and spasmed as she removed it from her neck and gently placed it in Atlas's hand. The key looked as if it lay on his porcelain skin for a second before it passed through his hand like air. It felt as a normal key would, pointing down and clanging on the blacktop before lying still. Atlas leaned down and put his finger on the key, and it passed through to the ground. Texas looked at the woman who mouthed back to her, "Pick it up".

Texas obeyed, leaning down, glancing up at Atlas several times before grasping the holdy bit and rubbing it between her fingers to verify its material nature.

"Texas, I will need you too, not just the key." Atlas said bluntly.

Fred ran between them. "No." He said.

Sheriff Plain moved him to the side.

"I need to speak with Ms. Rhodes first." Said the Sheriff. He looked at Texas. "We have some bad news." his voice began, "Please, you'll have to come back to your house, it's your mother." Plain looked at Atlas, then the girl.

"I will call on you again." Atlas said before turning around and leaving.

But we can talk about that later...

"I forget you walk backward through life,
only seeing what is behind and never what is ahead."
[Katherine the Great (not the Russian one,
the woman in Florida)]

Later.

Fred wouldn't leave her side, but at a safe distance, as he was reminded when Texas screamed, "Leave me alone!" to any person who hugged her. The townspeople were in a fright; it was hard when one of their own had died. They had all come as one large group, like a pack of penguins that made sure the strongest were on the outside, while the fearful, the young, and sick were in the middle, which meant that in two days' time, most would have the flu from a sneeze that emanated from the midpoint and stagnated in the back of the Funeral home.

Sheriff Plain stepped forward; the rest stepped back, en masse, and stood in front of her. "You're grieving, and I'm sorry for your loss, Texas." he nodded his head to her, "We are a close community... I mean, we just love you... and we love Mary, loved, no love... maybe loved... yeah... And we love you both."

He hugged her one last time, and Texas stood wide-eyed, angrily. "Thank you," Fred said, putting his hand on the Sheriff's shoulder. The townspeople, twenty-one in all, took their seats behind them and, for the most part, avoided the two for the rest of the night.

The casket lay open with a stiff Mary lying peacefully inside, Texas shaking her foot, sitting in one of the polyester couches they had lining the walls, and Fred next to her, a book in his hand as comfort. "You can't spell funeral without fun!" He reminded her. She walked up and touched Mary dimly and let the moment take her, let the light fade, the sounds dissolve into her heartbeat, and let the fear come over her. It wasn't sadness; she was sad, it gripped her in waves, but now it was fear, a moment when she realized that what was will never be again. A strong hand touched her shoulders, rubbing them.

"She looks dead." A voice said. Texas didn't even clench her fist; she made no note of his words, just turned blandly. "You hear me? I said she looks dead," Atlas smiled. "Texas. Yes, she does."

"Aaa," Texas stood with a gaping mouth.

Atlas began, "That wasn't funny, was it? Damn, I have to work on my timing. It's my timing, right? That was the problem? Anyway, I'm going to get some food. Do you want anything?"

Texas looks at him blankly. Pindar walked up behind her. "He wanted to come with. I'm supposed to say sorry for your loss, and I have, as your employer, so thank you." And walked off.

"We never finished our conversation... I'm calling on you now," Atlas said. She let the moment take her again.

"I see you're upset; a bad joke will do that. I'm going to be blunt. I need you and the key. How does 500 million sound for it? But you need to make up your mind quickly. I've already been standing still for too long." Atlas stood upright.

"We'll take it!" Fred jumped in.

"Excuse me," Texas answered before two men walked in, one with a sword and tunic, the other in full plate armor. Texas just looked at them blankly, Bob taking a nip from his flask and Thomas standing to address the woman in front. "She was a lovely woman," he began. "She–"

"Yes." Texas said.

"Did you know her?" Thomas asked. "Yes... I'm her daughter."

"Oh, did Mary marry? That's an awkward phrase, you know two 'm's."

"No." Texas looked down.

"Well, you see, we were brought here..." Thomas continued.

"Thank you for coming." Texas interrupted, shaking his hand before making her way back to sit. Ignoring them and everyone else the rest of the night.

Texas put her hand against the key under her shirt and turned her back to everyone. Atlas, in the direction of Texas, put up a finger. "We'll do lunch." He said as he left.

Somewhere else

The students and academics who were working quietly in the Public University Library were quite content focusing on their own devices. They had quite forgotten the oppressive feeling on their chest that was brought about by an androgynous herm hiding in the corner of the first-floor workroom, looking through an old book of art. Herm shoulders would raise and lower with the temperature of the room and would often sneeze in a lyrical fashion. He blended right in with the other PhD's and first years.

Now, most first-year Doctoral students won't speak to anyone else as they are often working on something so minute and detailed that it's of little value to the world at large. And they often don't give away anything on paper because, outside of their love of paper, they are often poor. Yet the man at the desk next to him was packing up his things when he leaned over and shoved a newspaper in his face. "You want this?" the man asked the angel.

"No, I'm–" herm stopped hermself, the newspaper was from Somewhere, North Dakota, and was turned to the obituaries; at the top was a picture of Mary. Under it read: local nun dies in ND and leaves priceless books to local library. He looks at her picture and for a moment he remembers, it was as if a lead balloon fell upon herm shoulders and herm realized the effect herm has on mortals. Herm's chest felt like it was collapsing in on herm, as herm's legs crumbled to color in herm eyes, they danced with numbers to build shapes that first went to a point, a dot in space. Dots piled on one another to create a line, and lines piled on one another to create a plane. Planes piled on one another to create a cube and cubes piled on one another– the music was singing to herm, herm's body convulsed in ecstasy, and then it stopped.

Herm opened herm's eye to everyone watching herm, the last 'ah' of a scream that had shattered the large framed window on the second floor escaped, his hands gripping the wooden desk so hard that his finger indentations were seared into the lacquer.

A man in a uniform was walking over, his hand on a taser that was at his waist. Raphæl looked over and said calmly, "I'm okay, sir. Thank you, thank you, everyone! Did you hear that music!?" Everyone looked at him and shook their heads' no'. "You didn't hear the music!? Oh, you poor souls! How could you not hear that it was–"

“Sir, ma’am? Sir? Professor...” The guard finally settled on. “Are you okay?”

“Oh, I’m better than okay!” Herm looked down at the paper and saw Mary’s face again. “I’m going to a funeral!”

“Professor?” Everyone was still staring.

“I’m going to a funeral!” Herm ran up to the guard and kissed him long and hard. “I’m going to go now.”

“You’re going to go.” The guard echoed.

“Yes, because I’m going to a funeral, oh happy day!” Herm exclaimed.

Back at Nowhere, ND

Texas was leaving the funeral parlor with Fred in tow, head down and numb. She walked over to her bike and looked at Fred. She put her hand over her chest and felt the key. She stopped and looked at him. “What do you think this thing does? It’s connected, right? And why does that guy, Atlas, want it so much? That’s not-“

“Doesn’t matter!” Fred said. “He will set us,” He corrected, “you, up for life.”

“But it does something for him.” She whipped around to Fred. “Follow me!” She said, jumping on her bike.

Fred jumped on his, screaming, “Wait!”

They made it down Main Street and to the center of town in less than a minute to hear Gabby whaling on his horn.

Texas got off and started walking in one move, throwing her bike to the ground. “Where have you been!? You came down and ate breakfast and.... And... all of this started with you!”

“It started with a question, Texas. It started when you asked a question.” Gabby said, putting down herm horn.

Texas sat down in front of herm. “Let’s say all this is true, that you are my guardian angel and that this, this key-“

“Careful with it.” Gabby interrupted.

“That this key is something special, that I somehow threw up. What is it? Why are you here, heralding the end of the world?”

"That is the key that unlocks everything. It runs everything."

Fred jumped off his bike, and his knees buckled and he dropped slightly in stature. Texas took a labored breath, "What do you mean runs everything?"

"All the machines that make the world go round." Gabby smiled.

"And what should I do with it? Huh, Gabby?" Texas exclaimed.

"That is not up to me to know. That is why it's so special."

"But, what would you like me to do with it?" Texas spat.

Gabby stood up and put down herm horn. The gravity was pushing on her and Fred, whose knees had bent, and he was down on all fours. Texas bared the weight and walked one step closer. "What would you have me do with it."

"I would have you unlock the closet." Texas stopped. "What closet?"

"The one God hide away in." Texas took a step back. "Explain."

"You are isolated from the world. There was a time when God walked the Earth. When you could hear the music, a pulse, a reverberation. It was clear. It's hard to hear anything now; we have trouble."

"We?"

"The other angels and I. I would have you open the closet and let God out; that would fix everything. That is what I think." Gabby looked down, disappointed.

"When I open it up, what happens?" Texas ran her fingers over the key.

"The best things. You will hear the music. All will hear the music and all will be right.

Sadness will be gone; happiness will rejoice. You would have full access to God." Gabby threw herm arms in the air.

"Your mom." Fred said quietly.

"And heaven." Texas said. "I could see people who passed-"

"Well, yes, but I mean God can't bring people back from the dead."

"Yes. My mom said God can do anything." Texas said to herself. "I don't think you understand God then."

"How do I get to the closet?" Texas was manic, pulling the blue glasses from her face and running her fingers through her hair.

“I want you to open the closet, but not like this. I won’t tell you.”

“Then I’ll do it on my own. You said there are more of you out there. And Atlas-“ Texas paced and clawed at her chest, a need pushing her forward, her mind pacing, her feet racing, her hair ablaze.

“Don’t give it to him!” Gabby dropped to herm knees and pleaded.

“Atlas has to know something about it.” Texas said hopping on her bike and left. Fred too hopped on and left, leaving a Bewildered Gabby behind.

THE NUMBER 7

"Did you ever think that god prays to humans as much as humans pray to him for peace?"

[Peggy, Mississippi, USA]

There was a smell to the house, stagnant air crept through the place, lingering like an uncle, two weeks passed, and then he said he'd leave for home. Even though he has a nice home, he has chosen to stay with you, on the couch, eating your food, and using your shower- even your favorite towel. Texas was sitting at the dining room table, fenced in by books from all realms of religious corners, ranging from the esoteric to the absurd, as she hunted for any mention of a closet.

Fred had been rooting through the kitchen and came up with a frozen lasagna Mary had made a week before her passing and was in the middle of cooking it through while tasting a half-opened bottle of wine on the counter. "It wasn't real. Gabby isn't some angel, he, herm, whatever, isn't anything." Fred said between gulps.

She slammed the book closed and started pacing before smelling the bubbling cheese clawing its way past the stagnation and wrapping itself around her.

"I found lasagna in the freezer; I thought it would be good," Fred yelled out to Texas.

"No!" Texas said, leaping forward and pulling open the oven door. "She was saving that for Wednesday." But Wednesday wouldn't come for her. Fred entered the dining room and stepped close.

"Get away from me," Texas demanded. "I'm okay." She held the water in her eyes. "What do I even do now, Fred?"

"I don't know." Fred stammered. He sat down with her, tried to reach out his hand as their fingers touched, she pulled back - "I don't believe in angels, or God, or any of that. I think there are some strange people who, all things considered, Mary could always attract. What I do know is that key, whatever it is, a man is willing to give you a lot of money for it." Fred pulled the seat closer to her. "Take the money and run. Let's go travel the world, eat, sleep, drink everything life has to offer."

Texas didn't say anything but just kept tapping her finger against the books slowly as if pushing something down.

There was a knock at the door. Fred waited for Texas to move, but she didn't. "I'll get it." He said.

A second knock happened when Fred said "Hello?" before he opened the door to witness two knights in full attire, hats in hand.

"Yes. Hi. My name is Father Thomas Aquinas, and this is Bob from the Inquisition. I mean, we're both from the Inquisition. It's not like I'm Thomas, and this is inquisitor Bob." He shuffled as Texas walked over. "We were at Mary's funeral. I used to know her, in the biblical sense, because the collar, of course, she was a good woman. You see, we didn't mean to be here, but we had a sign, we were following a bird that shat." They looked past Fred to see Texas slowly walking over, and they stopped. They saw the key around Texas's neck.

Fred stared intently at them, not knowing how to take it all.

Bowing slightly, "I'm sorry for your loss." Bob said and as they were making their introductions, before he could explain their meeting, a heaviness pulled on their shoulders, their heads filled with lead, and for a moment, they stopped breathing.

"Hello! What a wonderful morning," Raphæl started skipping up the front steps. Herm was androgynous in nature, a mix between boyish charm and feminine grace, a scarf pulled around herm neck and a corduroy jacket loosely hanging off herm shoulders. "This is a lovely house! Is this the place where the woman died?"

Everyone stared at herm.

"Not another one," Texas said to herself.

"Ah, yes, it is! Look at those almost tears and sorrowful looks, death death death was here. How wonderful! So, tell me, where is she?"

"I'm sorry, who are you here looking for?" Fred asked.

"I'm here for Mary; she died, right?" Raphæl said, barging past and up the stairs.

"Well, she's dead," Texas explained.

"Right, I know that, I'm not disputing it." Herm made herm way back down, "But I need to talk with her." Raphæl said, walking into the living room and taking a seat in a pink arm chair. "Yes, she liked this seat. I can still feel her warmth."

The squeak of brakes broke the moment, a shiny new sedan pulled up in front, and from it came a white, glistening figure complete with shades and a linen suit.

"This is her home. How lovely, it's the perfect size for the beginning of the revolution. So, tell me what she is like?" Raphæl continued admiring the geometry and looking at the cornice work as he walked in.

Texas walked out on the porch as the others walked up the front walkway. "Mr. Atlas, I'm sorry about before."

"No, it's okay. We have to keep moving, or people might catch up with me. But here, a golden parachute!" He said, pulling out a gold color tarp, "I brought one! It's not real gold, of course, because it wouldn't be useful. You know accounting for the weight and the density of the material, but it's gold color. I hope that works for you. It's a symbol. 500 million is a new number that I think you will like."

"No, no, it doesn't. I think you should leave." Texas said, realizing that to Atlas, none of this, her feelings, her time, her... everything didn't matter.

Atlas held up a dollar and winked at her, "Ah, you too know it's just all made up, too, huh?" Just then, a chair was thrown through the front window of Mary's home, the one made of velvet and lace, pink in color, that was still warm from Mary's buttocks. Through the jagged shards that still clung to the wooden frame was Raphæl and his unblinking eyes, with a finger pointing to Atlas. "How dare you be out here awake, in the sun, on the earth, with your fingers and toes! How dare you!" Herm proclaimed before lunging at him.

Atlas held out his arms in defense as their bodies collided with such force that the humans standing were all blown off their feet, and a small crater was produced around the place where Atlas had last stood. Atlas grabbed the angel and, with might and fury, threw herm through the upstairs window before running inside chasing after his prey. Texas jumped to her feet and ran inside, her ears ringing and chest near collapse, which prevented her from hearing a pleading Fred on his hands and knees, grasping at air as if he could hold on to her shirt and prevent her from going in.

Texas ran to the kitchen a moment before Atlas was thrown through the ceiling, landing on the kitchen table. Raphæl jumped through the hole and on top of Atlas, wings spread open, as the sounds of children singing echoed from the sky, and Texas dropped, the glory of the angel shown around her, and for a moment she thought she heard a tune, a melody lost to her something-- but it was gone and she was lesser for it.

Raphæl pulled hermself up with herm fist clenched, ready to hit Atlas, but he feigned and rolled to the right. "Get out!" Texas screamed before Atlas's body crashed into her, rolling her to the floor and pinning her against the wall.

"Vile, you should not be here; this is not part of the plan!" Raphæl spat.

"How would you know the plan?" Atlas retorted.

"You were cast out! You, with your differences between your legs, only we pure creatures were to usher the monkeys into the new era. Your time has gone."

Atlas lunged at Raphæl, pushing him through the wall and leveraging him to the ground with a single arm. "Foul! Your kind should be locked away until--"

Atlas took Raphæl's face and bounced it off the floor until the wood struts splintered and gave way to the basement. Fred was now at Texas's side, grabbing her arm, a terror ran across his face. "I can't lose you, too!" He cried but was blown back as Raphæl's wing burst through the hardwood, Atlas hanging onto his leg, being brought up by a wind that wrapped Texas in warmth and caressed them to sleep. Fred fell limp until a gust blew them both back to the moment.

Bob and Thomas had run in, picking up Fred and Texas, dragging their bodies from the house, arms around their chests, lifting and pulling until a heaviness hit them, a weight that didn't push or pull, it didn't sink and lift but as if a dark star was being born from inside, they all turned to watch Raphæl and Atlas in a final embrace, light emanating between them as their hands intertwined in a force like the world has not seen since its birth. There, they pushed as two continents caught in midair. Fred lunged at the remnants of the kitchen table, pulling it in front of them before the light turned to fire and fire turned to power, emanating, tearing through walls and structures, blowing the gang of four from their place and through the wall to the front lawn.

Bob grabbed Texas's arm, yanking her to the ground, pulling her to Atlas's car, and throwing her in the back seat before going back and picking up Thomas, lifting him into the passenger seat. Fred lay torn and limp on the lawn, and Bob looked to see if Fred's chest was moving, but it was still. Bob reached out for Fred to grab his body, but Atlas had lunged toward Raphæl. Bob made a choice; he got into the driver's seat and took off. Texas watched from the back window, pounding the glass, ripping at the seat, screaming "Fred" before the house collapsed and was out of sight.

Bob looked over to see Thomas, a large plank sticking out from his abdomen, doubled over, clutching the board with his left hand while his right hand had his phone out, dialing. "What are you doing?" Bob screamed.

"We have to talk to Bishop Illios," Thomas said. "You have to tell him the closet is real, they were angels, angels...and we found a key."

"We have to get you to a hospital!?" Bob uttered.

"No, we have to get to the safe house," Thomas said.

Atlas emerged from the debris and was on the run again.

A minute later, a woman in white with two clanking, full plastic gas cans in her hands that thumped up and down on her thighs, ran up to the mess. "Excuse me!" She yelled to an androgynous person in torn tweed, slowly walking down the path that once led to a quaint cottage. Herm didn't respond.

Luna paused at the destroyed house, making notes, but knowing this is what happens sometimes. "Excuse me. I'm looking for a black sedan. I would like to set it on fire." She said.

"I think we can help each other," Raphæl said.

Fred opened his eyes, and wood shards were stacked on the ground, and his chest was collapsing. He could feel the tendrils of life leaving him like a cord being pulled away, the browning out of his existence, and then a bright light, a brilliant, blinding light, overcame him, and he closed his eyes as a heaviness pressed upon his chest. "Herm's got this," Fred heard before he lost consciousness.

He felt his body lift up toward the sky and euphoria take him as his head sank back.

.

We're on number 8

"Wouldn't it be funny if we spelled Prometheus's name differently each time and never addressed it throughout the novel?"

[Felix Von Bruder]

Deep in the halls of the dark and shadowed land of the Vatican was the ornate bed frame of Bishop Illios. His phone was ringing, and he picked up. "Oh God!" The voice on the phone stuttering and stifling, the man's words squeaked and moved–"What do I do?"

Illios put on his glasses and made the sign of the cross. "My child, who is this?" He pulled back the phone to see 'Thomas' scrolled across the screen. "Thomas? Is that you? You sound so much younger?" Bishop Illios responded.

"I don't know..." To someone, the voice muttered, "It's Bob." The voice said into the phone.

"I don't know a Bob." The Bishop stood and put his finger in his ear, wiggling it gently. "Robert, From the store?" The Bishop asked.

"No! Father Robert. I am... I am working with Father Thomas."

"Oh, yes, Bob! Why would you call yourself Robert? I know you as Bob." The Bishop walked to a window to look up at the sky.

"What?" Bob gave up. "I think, Thomas. I think he is dead."

Bishop Illios stopped for a minute and waited. "So, you're looking to take over his job?"

"No!"

"Then I think it should go through the proper channels. I'm like your boss's boss." Illios pulled the phone out, but before he ended the call, he heard-

"He's dying." The voice on the phone said.

"Then take him to a hospital." His finger hovered over the end button and-

"I don't think you understand. He said the closet is real. There were angels-" Bob continued.

"Well, I bloody well... wait. The closet? He told –"The Bishop stiffed. "Do you

have a… key holder?"

"Yes!" Bob screamed.

"Does she know where the closet is?"

"No."

"Holy Christ, Saint Maria Grazia! Where are you?" There was a wet thud from his window. A frog, now gently pressing against the glass, was croaking in glee as another wet smack pained the glass.

"Thomas is dying!" Bob's voice rang out.

"We're all dying." The Bishop snapped to the moment again. The closet. He thought. "Where are you?"

"I don't know!" Bob looked outside at the barren waste that is North Dakota. "I'm in North Dakota."

"Then head to Our Lady of the Gray Church in Fargo. And Bob, you know what you need to do." The Bishop said, he pressed end and scrolled through the names on his phone. He came to the bottom and pressed send on a last name. "Hello?" the Bishop said, squeezing the phone. "It's Illios. We need to meet. We have a lead on a key holder. One of my agents said the closet is real."

And frogs rained from the sky. "I thought they were supposed to be Toads?" were the Bishop's last words.

They pulled up to the Lady of the Grey Church, a boring name in itself, but one that the catholic church thought fit the grey stone, baroque Gothic structure. It sat upon a hillside of a dense deciduous forest, hidden behind a mile and a half driveway that was seldom used. Bob had stopped the car from swerving but hadn't stopped his hands from shaking. "My house! My house! Why are you going here? Who are you? What is going on!?" Texas blurted out, repeating over and over without listening for an answer. This was going on for an hour of repetition.

The car slid to a stop at the front door of the convent just as the sky appropriately opened, letting rain hail down on them and pushing their tires forward. Bob jumped out and ripped open the passenger door as a beautiful, soft nun rolled a stretcher out, several followed behind her and grabbed Thomas, heaving him up. "No, don't help." She said, pushing Bob away, two more women in habits ran to the first woman's side and lifted the old man onto the stretcher. Texas stepped out of the car, and Bob's hand reached out, kindness and assurance, but was pushed away as Texas moved through the main doors. "Holy Mother Mary..." He said quietly.

In the back of the Abby, in the Southernmost corner, was a room fitted with a series of hospital beds in what looked like a recovery room. Convalescence room. Yes, a convalescence room with a rocker in the corner and the smell of antiseptic coating... Well, you have to keep it clean. I understand. Coating the walls as a thin layer.... We have a lot of elderly nuns. I mean, outside of Felicity, we haven't had a new sister to the order for twenty years. It's a dying order, so here it is: the elderly take care of the elderly, and sometimes we need an area to look over various bruises, cuts, and the like. Plus, the nearest medical facility is the county hospital, like... Your voice is grading. That's grating. Like it grates on you, like a cheese grater... Thank you. As I was saying. But–Now, I must ask you to leave. This isn't your story. Pardon me, sometimes the characters add themselves into the story to talk about extraneous bits.

Please note, reader, it's like this in all minds. Something we have a thought, or character in my case, that was not our own. So, go do that thing you think you can't do.

As I was saying~

By the time Bob had reached the infirmary, Thomas was convulsing and flailing. It was no use; Bob had seen what death looked like and thought it would be best to at least be at his side. Texas stood in the corner, arms folded, taking everything in until Thomas's hand wrenched up and pointed at her. The nun walked over and escorted Texas to his side, where they leaned down. "What? What is he saying?" she asked.

Bob pushed his way to Thomas's side with everyone else. "You," Thomas began, "I'm dying. You have the key, you are... You are the answer to the Inquisition. We are the first of our order. Before the church, we looked for the closet. St. Peter's descendants want to find it to close it; others want to open it. I don't know what's best, but you have the key. You have the key, you have the key, and I believe in reasons, not dice."

"Wait a minute!" Bob said, clenching Thomas's hand. "Thomas, she can't be in the order, it's a man's thing, right? Besides, she's like seventeen!"

"I'm eighteen." Texas reminded him.

"Really, now!?" Bob said, staring at Texas before standing up.

"I'm dying. I don't think I'm getting better. Bob, show her the way." Thomas said, ushering Bob back in.

"Like hell! I don't know the way. You said no one knew where the closest was, no one knows the way." Bob spat.

"You have to find it. I'm still dying, please leave me alone. Wait. You must find it. Not, half assedly like I was. You actually have to find it."

"But Thomas." Bob protested.

"Bob, I'm dying, fetch me some tea." Thomas said, taking a large, dramatic gasp.

Bob looked at the nuns before running out. He ran to the back of the convent, "Kitchen?" He shouted louder than he wanted. "To the left down the hall." One nun said.

Bob arrived and turned on the kettle before pacing back and forth, biting his thumb. He scrambled through the cupboards for a mug and tea, and by the time he found some, the water was boiling. He poured it full and let the tea soak for a minute before returning to Thomas's side.

Thomas grabbed the cup. "This is good tea."

"Thank you," said the pretty nun taking in a large whiff. "It's herbal, from what we grow on the ground. Bob leaned in close. "Thomas, tell me what to do now, please."

"Thomas, what am I supposed to do?" Texas blurted out. "Can't you see I'm dying." Thomas reiterated.

"Well, quite honestly, you've been dying the whole way from Nowhere to Fargo." Texas stated.

"Excuse me." A slender man said from the doorway, adjusting his shoestring tie and fine black suit. "Thomas?" Thomas nodded. "Hi, I think you're going to need a hug." The man said.

And with that, Thomas passed on.

Chapter 8, again?

"Dinosaurs existed, that's all I'm saying."

[Xia]

Fred woke up in the arms of an angel high above the ground, freezing and gasping for oxygen. Raphæl looked down and smiled, "Oh, you're awake!" Herm said, eyes unblinkingly focused on the horizon.

Fred turned his head and panicked, moving up and down, left and right, and fell; Raphæl snatched him from the air and fumbled with him as Fred's head faced up and down, screaming and flailing like a goose on Christmas. "If you calm down, you won't fall," Raphæl said before a woman's scream cut through the air.

Fred looked up to see Raphæl's face wreathed in glory, glowing as herm's skin emanated light. The scream cut through again. "And you," herm said to Luna on herm back. "Everyone must calm down."

Fred clutched herm tight, grasping onto Raphæl's long, flowing hair. The reality set in, and he began... "What was that? Who was that? What are you? You're an angel! Why haven't you revealed yourselves!? My side, it's..."

"Yes, I healed you. And yes, because there is a plan." Raphæl said plainly.

And Fred's memories flooded back: Texas, her mother, the house, his life. "A plan? For what? For her to die, for her mother's house to be destroyed?"

"Yes, yes, a thousand times yes. Don't take things so personally. A cookie once told me life is change." Raphæl smiled. "I'm not sure if I translated it properly in my head. A cookie is the tall one, not the short one, right?"

Fred wasn't listening; he relaxed his grip and sank into herm's arms, looked down, and screamed. "This is pleasant for me." Raphæl said, taking Fred and holding him close. "Come," herm said, "We are going to find our friends."

"I'm trying to sleep!" A voice cried out. The woman is the gas cans peeked her head over Raph's shoulder stabbing her eyes at Fred before once again taking a quite cozy position between herm's wings.

WE FORGOT CHAPTER 12

"If you're not lost, then you're found.
If you are found, your job is to get lost again."

[A proverb of the lake]

Enter a villain, Uranus, garbed in all blue jeans and a tee-shirt, with thin-rimmed glasses and boat shoes, made his way to and walked up to the shambles that was the house, surrounded by fluttering yellow caution tape. He ducked under the thin plastic line and let his eye follow a faint trail of blood that dotted the grass from the porch to the line. He walked up half the stairs to the porch and through a blown-out window that was now an empty door. "HHMMM?" He asked himself, running his hand along the frame.

He made his way through the front hallway, but as he moved towards the kitchen, he felt his legs stiffen. He dropped down and, with a slow, deliberate slap, clasped his chest and pulled on his shirt. He could feel their residual stillness, a deep longing in the air, and he took his knee and lifted himself back up.

He walked to the living room to see it obliterated, long black lines covered the floor, and cheese had holed the walls, save four small indentations where a chair had been. He walked out to the cratered lawn, picked up what was once a pink chair, and moved it back to the center of the room. He walked in front of the chair and could feel the hair on his arm raised as static charges danced from tip to tip. He clasped the arms of the chair.

He took a deep breath and willed his voice, deep and resonant, in a middle C he let out a long EEE. Nothing. And once again, he took a breath, and in a middle C, he gave an EEE, and for a moment, there was a person in the chair.

"Ah, there you are. I thought someone was there."

He once again took a breath and bellowed out an EEE followed by an AAAAA and willed his being to the moment, feeling every sense to that moment he was in and started whispering, "That's it. Listen to my voice. Listen to the sound of my voice, I am here." He took a moment and looked up to see a faint blue glow emanating from the chair.

He tethered his mind to now. "Hear the birds, nothing exists outside of their moment.

Listen to my voice, feel the chair, deep in its seat, soft against your skin, there– "And there was Mary sitting on the chair, breathing heavily.

"That's it. Listen to my voice." Uranus said in a slow, mellow tone. "The air is burned, smell it, feel the air move from past the hairs inside of your nostrils, and feel the carbon on your skin."

She came more into focus and opened her eyes.

"Who are you?" She asked, a kind smile came across her face as she leaned forward. Her eyes moved to a cross on the wall, and she winked out and back in.

"Oh, hello." She said.

"I was here to kill someone." Uranus gently said, patting her arm.

"What?' She blinked out of existence and back in. "No, I'm okay, would you like some tea?" She tried to stand up, rocking back and forth, but couldn't move.

Uranus thought about it and said, "Yes." He moved the remnant seat, spitting with ethereal flames, to the place where the table had been. Trying to marry two broken ends and turning over a fallen chair, he sat with her. He mimed picking up a teapot and pouring it into a mug, and she reached out to where his hands were. Between her fingers, a mug appeared, which she grasped and drank from. Uranus poured himself another glass of tea from a mimed teapot to an imaginary cup and pretended to pick it up.

"Oh dear," Mary said. "It looked like you didn't have tea."

Uranus looked kindly at her. "Imagine I do. Imagine it is in your best mug with steam pouring from it."

"I don't understand. That won't give you tea."

"It has to begin in the mind first, Mary. For you, you are in a place where it is all mind.

Think it, and it will be." And with his words, a mug appeared, blue in hue with steam pouring from the top.

"I'm sorry, but I don't have anything else. Would you like some water?"

"No, tea is good, thank you. So, I need to know where a woman with red hair can be found."

"Oh, you must mean my daughter. I'm not sure, she left after... I died, didn't I?" She winked out of existence again.

"Feel the soot touch your skin. Listen!" He took a breath and intoned EEE in middle C. "Your hair against your chair, the velvet fibers pull against each strand~"

And she was back in place.

"Where did you go? Never mind." Uranus said softly. "I don't know, I can't remember. I think–"

"No! Don't. You must stay here, focusing your mind and feeling where you are, listening to the moment. Remember you are in the place of thought, the realm of forms."

"Why?"

"You're dead."

"Oh, I know that's silly. I'm waiting for my light but~" She paused. "Why am I still here?"

"It's been a tough couple of days for the powers that be. They will get to you. But you must stay here, don't let your mind wander. Your consciousness is not tethered to a physical body, so you are no longer bound by this space and time."

"No longer bound? As I can go anywhere?" There was a tinge of excitement in Mary's tone.

"Yes, sort of. You could, but if your consciousness is tethered to another body in another time, you will be brought back to that life."

"Back to that life?"

"Yes, in a way. You have lived many lives. This life was but a passing. If you go back in time, you go back to the life you were in at that time." Uranus explained as ethereal blue glasses appeared on his face.

"Oh, that's lovely. But what are you doing here? This place. Are you here to take me to my light?"

"No, I am not that. I need your daughter, tell me about her." "It's been how many days? Since my death."

"One."

"Exactly, and they can't even pick me up."

"That is the reality of life."

"And you, how do you know all this? Are you human or..." she paused and smiled, excitement building again, and the divine crept in. "Are you... not human?" Mary questioned.

"I am not. I am one half of a..." He stopped and looked down. "I need to ask you, were the angels here?"

"I don't know," She looked around. Her house was in shambles. Fifty years of love and kindness, of family... she should have screamed and cried but now, here, her feelings were not the same. She thought of Texas. She didn't see her. Then she blinked, and she was by the shore walking, a blinding light, enneagon upon enneagons, nine in sides, convex and concaved – blended.

Mary felt happy, a child, crying in her arms, with toasted red hair, the sun was too bright, and there was... She was back to the man singing an E.

"Here now." Uranus said.

"I was dead before this happened. But there was one, he was nice, we had breakfast." Mary said.

"Where is her key?"

"Oh, she had a lovely key. My darling Texas. By beautiful daughter. I put it around her neck-"

A tall man in a black suit walked into the doorway and pulled out his clipboard. He cleared his throat and let his footsteps echo across the wooden floor.

"Pardon, I don't mean to interrupt. This is touching, but I'm looking for a Mary Rhoades."

Mary stood up, "Oh, that's me!"

The man in black gave Mary a hug, and she felt love, the gravity of love, the lightness and contradiction of love. She felt 1 + 1 = 1.

The man in the suit licked the pencil in his hand and put a check on the paper before him. "And you are?" He said, looking at Uranus.

"Doesn't matter," Uranus replied.

"I don't see your name on the list." The man in black said.

"I do not think you are here for me."

The man stood closer and smelled the air. "Are you?"

"Yes. I'm sure I am whoever you think I am." Uranus dismissed him.

"Oh, good! I'm glad you're involved. Metatron will be very pleased. You know she is looking for you. Your better half. I don't see much of her anymore thanks to the humans." The man in black said, his eyes retreating to the clipboard and writing notes.

Thomas walked up behind the man in the black suit. "I know-" He blinked out of existence again.

"Oh no." The man in the suit said.

Thomas snapped back, "There was a fight, and I died."

Uranus started singing a high E as he edged his way to the door frame. "Were you here with a girl..." Uranus tilted his head and felt. With red hair?"

Thomas blinked out, and Uranus sang more, his voice straining, eyes scowling down. "Where is she?" Uranus demanded.

Thomas blinked in. "At the Grey Lady."

Unperturbed, the man in the suit was ushered aside by Uranus. "Now, we are backed up, Mary. I'm going to need you to come with me." He said.

"Thomas?" Mary said.

"Mary? It's been ages! I was at your funeral; I met your daughter. She was here-"

Uranus bent down and grabbed some earth that had been flung from the lawn among the debris, chanting in a low tone.

"Ah, no, you can't do that. Not here. No!" The man in black said, moving away.

There was a silver chord entwining Thomas and seemed to wink in and out without a second thought.

"You will take me to your friend," Uranus demanded.

"Metatron will hear of this." The man in black said, scratching something onto his pad. "Come, Mary."

"But–" And the man in black and Mary vanished.

Uranus walked over and took the cord wrapped around Thomas. "Come, we too have something to do."

Chapter lost in the forest again - here.

"There is a spike in anxiety when you think of a thought that is not your own. It is your job to weed them out and, like a balloon, watch them float away."

[A red balloon that was trying to be a plastic bag]

The view from The Grey Lady wasn't more than it sounded. Misting rain flitting across a rose window in the center of a Gothic nunnery, outlining a six-hearted floret center among saints and leaded light. "We're investigating it." Sheriff Plain said over the phone.

Texas spun, "You don't understand! Fred–" The Sheriff interjected, "Texas. Are you safe?"

She looked around. There was a nun across from her holding Texas's hand, and another nun with charcoal features who brought over a cup of tea. Her hand lightly grazed Texas's as she laid the mug in her free hand, which brought a smile and a slight head nod with condolences from the sister.

"I'm safe," Texas said.

The Sheriff took a deep breath and slowly asked. "Good, where are you?" The nun with the mug whispered, "The Gray Lady, Forks."

"The Gray Lady. In Forks." Texas repeated.

"I will come to call in three days. Until then, stay there, don't call or make contact with anyone." Sheriff said, the sounds of clanging and shuffling echoed on his side as...

"Fred! What about Fred, and the house!? What about Mr. Pin–"

"Texas, I will contact you in three days." And with that, the sheriff hung up.

The sun filtered through the stained glass projecting the face of a sleeping lamb onto the casket, fitting for on this day where they held the memorial for Father Thomas, his body would not be taken to his hometown of Bengough, Saskatchewan and laid to rest in the tiny cemetery outside of town between a body of a repentant thief and Mrs. Hammon and her nine mummified cats she has buried with her for protection in the afterlife. Rule 3 of an Inquisitor: he will be buried here, for that is where he passed.

Bob was digging the dirt from under his nails as the sword he carried around, scraped and scuffed, and was missing a tip after cutting wood, and now sat on the pew holding the sacramental wine, making the sign of the cross before saying "the blood of Christ" and taking a large swig from the bottle. At this point, he was too into his prayers to hear the few small steps of Felicity Hum, the youngest nun in the abbey and free of the stretcher we had when she first rested her eyes upon Bob. Her steps were as air and walk was more of a slide as she blew in the back of the church and sat down next to Bob. She folded her hands and rocked a little, saying a prayer; her stoic face burst into a grin, and she opened her mouth and faced Bob as if to say something. After taking a look at his face, she took a breath and became once more stoic.

"Bishop Illios wouldn't like this, and this' taking the wine from his hands 'is for the nuns." She said and pulled a flask from under her skirt. "I took the liberty of refilling this with 18-year-old Bourbon from my own stash. I heard it was your favorite."

He took a nip. "Well, this–hint of apple?"

"Pomegranate." She said.

She looked around and saw that the place was empty and took the liberty. She leaped up a little and put her hand on his shoulder, her face inches from his. "Is it true you're from the Inquisition?"

Bob stopped and stared at her for a while, pretty, in a girl-next-door, sweet face, light and soft, the beginning of smile lines around his lips, but he turned to his mentor, lying peacefully in the casket, and said, "Serves you right." And with that, he stood up, pushing her to the side, and headed to the door. Felicity jumped and bounded after him, taking a discreet distance from his left as they made their way down the cloisters. She clasped his taught should feeling the muscle and sinew from the years of carrying a sword. "So, it is true? That is why Bishop Illios called here, why you came here with a dying priest. Did you find something? Did you find the closest?"

And with that word, Bob stopped dead in his tracks, turning to her, clasping her shoulders, "What closet?"

"You know, the closet. The Inquisition that has been looking for the closet. I know you know."

There was silence.

"That is what the Rosicrucians said. They say there is no such thing, and that no one is a part of it, even though they have followers across all of Europe. I heard the Inquisition went underground after the Middle Ages, something of a PR issue."

Bob released her and looked around. "We were in an accident. I don't know what this Inquisition is."

"I want in!" "Into what?" Felicity bounced in excitement.

She stared at him. Bob broke the silence: "Is there any news from Bishop Illios?"

"I don't know. I would assume Mother Superior would run down here if there was."

"Bob, what is going on!" Texas yelled, flinging the door open.

Later.

The memory of her home flittered in her head, but that was gone. Her mother's hand came into view, but that was gone. She could remember that one time Mom was in a wheelchair. She remembered her scent, but was it hers? Her face was always blurry.

Bob stood up slowly, Texas was now sitting in the pew with him and Felicity. Texas began again. "Bob, I need to know about the closet."

"I knew it!" Felicity said.

"No," Bob said plainly.

Texas walked up very close. "Bob, I lost my mother, my home, and friend, my–" Her hand balled up as she spit the words out between gritted teeth, grinding the emotions into enamel, "I figured it out. The closet will undo this." She finished with a tear hanging in the corner of her eye.

Bob looked at Felicity.

"Tell m–us!" Felicity piped in.

"Lower your voice! You are the one who brought this on to all of us." Bob said, pushing the palm of his hand down as if to hush everyone. "You want to know, fine."

Texas stared him dead in the eye. Bob looked around.

"Do you still have your key?" Bob asked. Texas clasped her neck and grasped it. She still had to key, but to what? The closet? "Put it in my hand," Bob said with his palm out.

Texas looked at Felicity and put the key in his hand. Without missing a step, he threw it in front of them. There was silence. Not a clank, not a bounce, not a sound. Texas lunged forward but stopped when Bob asked. "Now, give me the key."

"I don't have it," Texas said. They all stopped. "You do."

Texas squinted her eyes and slowly raised her hand up to her neck, and under her shirt was the distinct, hard shape of her key. She pulled it out.

"The key is yours," Bob let out a heavy sigh, "and always will be."

"And what does it open? It opens the closet, right?" Felicity said.

"Yes," Bob began.

Felicity dropped to her knees and began to pray. She looked up at Texas and said, "I don't even know where to begin! Please, this means she can open the closet?" Felicity hummed.

"Yes," Bob began, "But..."

"But, what?" Texas demanded.

"That is all I know," Bob said.

Felicity stood up. "Now, Bob," she said with a direct tone. "Tell us about the inquisition."

"That's what I was going to start with–" He started in a downward tone. "No, the myth! Not your personal story," Felicity interrupted.

"I was–"

"Like the point of it." She was bouncing eagerly.

"Yes, but–" Bob tried again.

"Just start!"

"STOP!" Bob stood up.

There was a moment of silence, and the ghosts in the corner stepped back slowly through the wall, the mouse tiptoed out, and a fly, who was tired of running into a window, decided to look casually out into the field, pretending it didn't hear anything.

Bob let out a long sigh, "Long ago," He began, "in a galaxy far~"

"Nope." Felicity demanded.

"You see, there once was a girl from Nantucket~" Bob continued, the Bourbon was talking.

"Fine!" Felicity cut him off.

Felicity cracked her neck and, in a long, drawn-out, exaggerated breath, she began, "Let me tell of the Inquisition. While the tower ~" she paused and leaned into Texas, "The tower of Babel," she explained, "~ was still up. The people of the world had a direct line to God and God's agents, also known as Titans. Well, one day he disappeared, no one knows why."

"Stop," Bob interjected.

"No, they don't. Well," Felicity continued, "they do? It doesn't matter. The Titans were left in charge, and they had arguments as to how humanity should continue, should they be directed as cattle, should they lead themselves, or should they be wholesale slaughtered. They were like us, petty, jealous, and so on. Somehow the angels came around, children, if you will. They fought the titans. I don't know." She stared at Texas, "These creatures, we called them titans. They were giants of men and women. The Inquisition was to find everything. That's why if you read Genesis, it says Elohim, plural. Because it was no longer the one true God, but God's representatives on earth."

"Just stop," Bob said flatly.

Felicity was putting the pieces together. "Bob. This isn't just a story."

She continued. "The Inquisition existed before the church. It was started by a group that is unknown to us. They were absorbed into the catholic religion, as they were into all religions, each sect reporting to a higher authority that keeps in contact with the powers that be. The holy persons tasked with finding the closet that God has locked himself in and the people who have a key, the key holders, like you. They are people who are born with keys, often inside of them."

Texas said. "That doesn't explain anything. Look, even if there is a God, some all-knowing thing, why would he put a key in me or other people? Why would he lock himself away? Why would his agents, or whatever you want to call them, not know the plan?"

"I know, right. It's all made up mumbo jumbo." Bob said. "Look, the Inquisition was Thomas and me, and we would run around the world drinking and hanging out. Most of the time, he would be reading old books in obscure languages. When I asked him about it, he would say, 'It's a wild goose chase, but we have to look busy.' That is what I know of the order. It is a wild goose chase. Every year, we would go to the monastery of the Inquisition and set out on the darkest path." He took a breath. "Until you, we had never met an angel, a titan, a key holder, anyone to do–but now. Now, we have this." Pointing to the key. "And I don't know where to go or what to do." He said slowly.

He stood. "I just don't know what to do." He looked up at the rose window and to the side leaded glass windows. There was a cross with a red sash draped and wrapped around the top with a flame above. He realized something. And he left.

Texas and Felicity waited there in awkward silence.

Felicity spoke first, "So, you're a key holder?"

Texas pulled out the key. "I threw this up the other night." Felicity looked it over. "It looks so plain."

Texas. "There was this person in the morning after that was sitting at my table, called him... no, it was hermself... an angel."

Felicity inhaled sharply. "Herm?"

"And my boss, well, my boss's boss, stopped by and fought another one that looked like that angel."

Felicity smiled at Texas, "Then you can save us. You can save all of us."

Texas smiled back. "But I don't want to. I just want to go home."

They heard chopping off in the distance as a sword was hitting wood.

Later

Bob wiped the sweat from his brow as he rolled his taut shoulders and stretched his bulging arms out, the right one still holding the sword, a little shorter and more damaged. His stomach contracted, and he walked to the kitchen, but didn't see anything in the fridge worth having. He pulled out a cross he had dangling around his neck and got down on his knees. "I know we don't talk, but let's face it, we don't like each other very much." Bob began his prayer, "But I'm calling in a favor. You owe me. And I want some good food, please, just let me find some good food."

There was a commotion and a reverberation off the stone, and a pounding could be heard through the halls. Bob stood up and made his way to its origins and arrived at the front door as the Mother Superior was making her way with two other nuns from the opposite hall. But as they get closer to the door that was being berated, their footsteps feel heavier, tougher to move, and stuck in pudding. Bob held up his hand to warn Mother Superior and signaled to her that he would check, but could barely lift his arm; the sword fell to the ground with a clank.

Bob mustered up the strength to take a step forward and clasped the handle, knowing that last time he felt this, Thomas died, that a house was destroyed, and creatures of terrible power...

He looked upon the guests. They had pizza, the door was open, Bob's hand clutched the handle, wet with sweat and red. Fred opened the pizza top lid, "Bob, right? I'm Fred. We met back at Mary's house. We brought Cheese and pepperoni." Bob looked over to the androgenous glowing gorgeous creature next to him. "Oh, right. This is Raphæl, whom I think you know, and Gabby, and this here is Michael." Michael was looking down and not making eye contact. "They're angels." Fred continued. "And this is Luna; she is not an angel."

Pizza, Bob thought. All prayers are answered in the order they are received.

Moments later, ten minutes or more.

The nuns were knocking on every door, waking and pulling each other to the main dining room. Mother Superior was clutching her rosary and pacing up and down the halls, watching as her wards lined themselves up to meet the Angels. Then the basement door opened, at first slowly to giggles, then a full laugh as Texas and Felicity popped their heads out and laughed uproariously at the aged nun.

"Sister Felicity," Mother Superior began. The two stumbled to the hall and shut the door behind them.

"Mother~" Felicity backed off.

Mother Superior's stern gaze kept eye contact. "What are you doing–"

"Thank you for understanding," and with that, Bob whisked the two away to the dining room, ushering Texas and Felicity with him.

Bob pushed Felicity and Texas into the room to find Fred, Raphæl, and Gabby eating slices. Fred dropped his piece and flung himself around Texas. "Oh, thank God you are alright! Thank God!"

Felicity dropped to the floor and cried, holding her hands together. "Angels!"

"Hi, I'm Gabby, and this is Raph. Do you want pizza?" Gabby smiling, herm eyes locked on hers. Felicity felt the first layer of skin move down her spine, reaching her toes and causing them to curl in, the nails near popping with blood.

"No, I... I... Devine." Felicity reminded them.

"So, are the rocks and trees. Now, come have some pizza with us." Herm took Felicity's hand, and a jolt of fire went up her arm; she retracted.

Texas wrapped her arms around Fred and kissed him, instinctively holding her lips against his. "You two are cute," Raphæl said.

Texas pushed him off. "I thought you were dead."

They embraced and held each other, and she let go as two beads trickled down her face before Bob walked over and announced to the room~

"I'm leaving. I think you all should, too." Bob interrupted and glanced at the rest.

No one moved. A nun knocked on the door, and Bob opened it to see a woman kneeling, shaking with her hands out. Bob looked back and reiterated, "Texas, you're coming with me."

"No," Texas said flatly, her spine stiffening before-

There was some hushed tones and whispers Bless us, bless us. He turned to "Gabby or Raphæl, the sisters were wondering if you could bless them?" The nun at the door said.

Gabby stood up. "I will," Herm said, standing up and making his way into the rectory.

Raphæl shoveled the last bite into his mouth, "We should be heralding the end of the world soon, right?"

Michael shuffled out, looking at the floor.

Bob walked out to God knows where.

Later

The last nun was being escorted out after the blessing of the laying of hands, their knees still weak, some still letting out long moans, while the angels looked over the iconography in amazement.

"I don't get it," Gabriel said.

"I know, I would think you would want something happy. I thought God was celebrating." Raphæl rubbed his hand over the stations of the cross.

Later.

Texas was gazing upon Fred, head slightly askew, his body limp and eye closed upon a cushioned seat outside the blessing. The room was a commotion, with black and white moving within and out of the double door that swung freely. Fred had a trail of drool making its way down the left side of his chin as Texas sat on the floor, looking up at him. Texas's hand shook a little. Fred was still alive; she smiled and bit her lip. She had to step out, quietly. She needed quiet. She walked through the corridors and came across an opening in the stone that led to a central courtyard covered in greenery. The moon cast her light upon the leaves and danced down to the blades of grass that shook from a cascading breeze.

Through the shrubs, Texas saw a ghost-like figure, veiled in a luminescent white that blended into her pale complexion. Texas distinguished her from the stone floor to the gentle earth and was greeted by a "Hi!" from between two branches.

Luna, still radiating in the night, peered her head around and smiled. "You're here too?" Texas looked her up and down. "You no longer have the gas cans on you."

"No, I do. I just left them outside. Don't want to burn down this place." She said, grinning.

Texas nodded not knowing what to say but landing on, "I'm Texas."

"I'm Luna. Nice to meet you."

There was silence.

Texas asked her question, the one that for her, set this whole thing in motion. "Why did you want to burn down Mr. Pindar's place?" Texas took a seat under a tree, and Luna sauntered over. She sat with her legs crossed and folded her hands pressing them together, playing with the air caught between her palms.

"Who is Mr. Pindar?" She said. The moon rained down and echoed across the open space, dashing around the oiled leaves of the courtyard.

"The man at the end of the road?" Texas said.

"The house at the end of the road?" Luna smiled a delicious grin before sinking her teeth into the question. "I don't know a Pinder. I was after Atlas."

Texas looked at her. "Why?"

"Because he's a nasty, vile man. He is like a stain that needs a good blotting." She said matter-of-factly. Texas raised an eyebrow. "Did you not recognize him?" Luna asked.

"I just want to go home. I don't know about any of this, or all of it." There was a pause as a bird landed on a branch, knocking one leaf from its bow. "I just want to go home." She repeated.

"You can't now. It's gone."

Texas felt the heaviness in her chest. "It's not gone." She squeezed her hands together and felt herself tighten. "It's not gone." She said again.

Luna leaned in. "It's gone. It never will be." And she leaned into Texas and hugged her.

And they sat in silence for the next twenty minutes as Texas let go of all that happened the day through small shakes and gobs of tears and heavy breaths.

Luna pressed in and felt something hard against her chest. She gently pulled back Texas and looked down the front of her dress to see the outline of a key. Plain and simple as her.

"I wish I had one. I would turn this place into a paradise." Luna said. "What do you mean?" Texas whispered.

"You can run a great machine, if you can pierce the vale that is. You're very special." Luna said before, once again pulling Texas and holding her. There was silence. Luna began again. "That's the one thing people don't talk about enough, the times we can't go back to."

Not much later, Luna had kissed Texas on the forehead, and without saying a word, she left the courtyard and Texas to her own under the tree. Texas's chest convulsed a little as she made her way to the corridor again and walked, hearing the muffled sound of her footsteps. Fred appeared out of the doorway and grabbed Texas, yanking her into the kitchen and pulling a chair out for her. "There you are! I was worried about you! What happened after the house?"

Texas snapped back to the present and hugged him. Fred was awkward and kept his hands at his side for a moment before embracing her. "What happened to you!? I thought you were dead! Where were you? What did the angels do? Did they bring you back from the dead? What–" Texas berated him.

"I was in a sex club, they locked up an angel named Michael, but Raphæl said they technically can't trap an angel, but Michæl seems to think they can. Raphæl said we need him for a battle, some big, woohoo battle, I don't know, they were being coy about it all. But, there is this woman who knew the angels like. This one is known as Astarte. She, well, she didn't–"

"You mean herm."

"No, apparently. I learned this. She was wearing a very revealing dress, and while angels are lacking in the genitalia, she was not." Fred raised his eyebrows while Texas winced a little. "And angels can just give orgasms, like through touch, apparently."

Texas was fixed on the word sex and hadn't been listening to the other parts. "It was weird. The world outside is weird. I really–"

"How was the sex club?" Texas asked, smiling, the blood running to her cheeks.

"I learned some moves." Fred tensed and looked down.

"You learned? Like someone taught you?" Texas shyly asked.

"No, I just watched." There was a pause again, always interrupting where it's not wanted. Fred turned. "We should go back. Talk to Sheriff Plain and figure–"

"I already did." Texas blurted out. "What did he say?"

"He said stay here. BUT I'm not going to! We have to find the closet."

"You lost me."

"The closet, look God hid himself away in a closet, and I have a key. This key." She pulled out the key from under her shirt. "We can reset everything."

"I don't think that is how this all works." Fred sheepishly stated.

"We have to go back to town and find the man with the wooden teeth." Fred looked at Texas. "Tomorrow. Tomorrow, we'll go."

They hugged and couldn't let go. Texas started sobbing, and Fred held her tighter, wrapping one arm around her waist and the other around her neck, kissing the side of her head, pieces of hair sticking to his tongue. As the sobs quieted, her body became heavy, the exhaustion took hold, and she was in pain all over. Her eyes drooped, and Fred whispered, "The nuns prepared us rooms down the hall. They aren't much, like small cells, but..."

Texas shook her head yes. And, with that, Fred walked her to her room, tucked her in, and shut the door before going off to his own room. Texas was asleep before she even hit the pillow.

In the rectory, after blessing all the nuns, the Angels sat looking up on the face of the rose window that resembled the geometric shape of 528Hz and saw images of the four angels, Michael, Raphæl, Uriel, and Gabreal, hewn in glass that stood at the points of the compass looking onto the rectory. "Those were the days. The four amigos." Raphæl said.

Gabby sat up straight and looked at his counterparts. "I think that Fred person is talking about us. Being around a key holder is new again."

"What do we do now, Raph?" Michael asked, staring at the floor.

"I think she will commit. We need the key bearer to drive the story. I heard the music, you know." Raphæl smiled raising herm's eyebrows. "The real music. Do you think it's already open?"

Michael lifted his head; Herm eyes wide and filled with tears. Gabby tilted herm head, trying to hear the strings of the universe that tie to the top of the head of a pin and bind each to every cause and effect. "I thought we made a promise." One of them said without speaking.

They paused and...

"No direct interference," they said in unison.

"But," Raphael continued, "that was only humans. We can directly interfere with Titans. If things get bad enough, she will choose to open the closet, then we will hear the music again."

There was another pause, a quiet one that grew louder. Their eyes flittered between one another as small heads shook, each angel ending in a yes. "If things get bad enough…" They said.

Around the same time.

Uranus walked along route 2, whistling a tune, well, trying to whistle, but as he did, his minor and majors didn't mix; the melody would jump too quickly, and the harmony could slap you in the face. Thomas's translucent form walked alongside him, listening with a wince~

"What are you singing?" Thomas asked. "I'm trying to remember a song."

"Ah, yes, that is the whole reason they invented the internet. That and nudes. Not that I would know anything about nudes." Thomas waxed. He was getting used to being a ghost, and his companion knew so much that it was like being in school again.

"No, this is not a song sung by you. This is the song that brought all things into creation. You know of this?" Uranus began. "This song, it is harmony, vibration, information. It was all."

"No, in the beginning God said let there be light. Now, you see God spoke, then it came into form."

"No. You humans–there was an awareness, then a thought, then a song. Yes, it began with a word, but the language was in song. It's like every mother said. It's not just about what was said but how it was said. It is a tonal language, it is the whole of language, that is if you were able to speak it, you could make the ocean retreat, the mountain rise, and~"

"And that is what you are after?"

"Me? No, I don't care about the power. Power is elusive; it is not something that can be tamed or controlled. It is fickle, and ultimately, power will only have power over you. No, this is not something anyone wants to have; that is why I want it. I am a part of the song, not the conductor. I am– To be a part…"

"Ahhh!" Thomas screamed, and his ghost flickered. He blinked back in. "Sorry, I was reliving my death."

"Yes, those emotional loops are hard to get through. It's harder when you are not tied to a body to keep in the moment. You flitter back and forth between time and place, which makes ghosts go crazy. Sometime from now, we shall find the girl. Where is your safe house again?"

"The Gray Lady in Grand Forks, North Dakota. I'm sorry I missed that. Who are you again?"

Uranus looked up to see a ball of flames in the sky.

When Numbers are Present

"Don't eat the yellow snow, but if you do, y
ou may need to seek help."

[Not real medical advice]

Earlier.

Texas was dreaming. She was at first on tough but firm ground, being bounced by what felt like three giants, but the ground gave way to stone. She felt as if she were placed upon an altar. She screamed, but no words came out. The sun overhead darkened too, and there were flies buzzing and swarming. In the distance, there was a tapping that was getting louder and louder as the night became colder, gripping her toes and contracting her muscles.

Texas felt her breath come in short bursts. There was a hand on her head. It was lovely. Then she was outside for a gathering. There were marshmallows, and chocolate, and a warm, cozy fire. She didn't see the faces, but it was a party. It felt like a party. There was some celebration, and she felt like they were all here for her. The images were blurry, and loving, and the place was warm, now hot, and too hot-

She opened her eyes and heard the crackling of a bonfire that she was sitting on top of. She was lashed to a board that sat on the stack of wood Bob had been cutting earlier that day. She felt the flames licking the sides as she screamed, "HELP!"

She felt her body loosen as the rope started burning, and the wooden board warped as the heat attached to the fibers. She rolled back and forth, yelling "HELP," but only heard the crackle of the fire and the dance of the flames taunting her demise. Then a lash snapped and smacked her in the face, her arms were free and wriggled up and down, pulling at the ropes that were on fire before finally escaping.

She rolled to the left, and the board came crashing down, sending embers flying, teasing her red hair, and singeing her face. "HELP!" She screamed again. This time she was on the ground, the grass cool and wet from the evening. She continued to roll until she was soaked from the evening dew and cold. She assessed herself, padding her body and head. Outside of frayed pant legs, she was whole.

"Texas!" Someone was yelling. She turned to see everyone rushing out of the nunnery from various doors as the flood lights turned on. "Texas!" It was Fred's voice. A choir of children could be heard in the distance moving at the sound of through until Michael, Raphæl, and Gabriel landed in front of Texas. "What happened?" Gabriel said.

"I was nearly burned alive!" She said, looking around. She looked back at the fire, and from the tree line, opposite the nunnery, came Felicity and Bob. A glint from the fire caught her eye as she saw his sword stuck in the dirt by the flames.

"Who did this!" Texas yelled at no one.

"Come with me, child." Mother Superior said, holding out her hand, pushing down on the air in front of her.

"No! Who did this?" Texas said.

"Did you ask another question!?" Bob said, walking up to the group gathered around her. "Did you ask another question?"

"What?" Fred said.

"What do you mean??" Texas reiterated.

"Did you ask another question! You're a key holder, you had to expect this." Bob said flatly.

"No, I did not expect this." Texas said. "How was I even dragged out..." She looked at the pile of burning wood. "Why were you in the woods?"

"Texas, my dear, come in." Mother Superior said.

"And where were you!" She said to Gabby, "You're my guardian angel, where were you?"

The angels looked at one another and shrugged, their lips turned down, eyes darting.

"We're here now." Gabby said.

"That's not good enough! And where were you!?" Texas said, staring at Fred.

"I don't know!?" Fred stammered.

"Where is Luna, that little pyro?" Texas screamed.

"Who?" Mother Superior said.

"Oh," Raphael began, "She didn't start the fire, she would have used gas, and you would have gone right up in flames." Herm said, shaking herm's head.

"Texas..." Fred meekly began. "Let's go inside."

"You ask another question, didn't you? I knew you shouldn't have been given any grace! You are a key holder. The inquisition's job was to stop the questions from being asked. Forget about the closet. Only bad things happen if you are looking for God. The inquisition would burn people like you at the stake; we should have done that to you." Bob looked at the pile of burning wood and back at Texas. Texas made a connection in her head.

Texas looked the dying firing, "Did you start this?" Texas barrel to Bob. "Did you start this!?"

Felicity stood between them. "Asking questions is dangerous."

Texas grabbed Felicity's shoulder and pushed her out of the way, and Felicity hit her in the face. Gabriel leaned in. "I didn't see that coming. I should have been there."

Felicity went back to Bob and held his hand.

"I have an idea!" Raphæl said. "We will guard, because we are guardian angels!" Herm said.

Everyone looked at them. Michael gave everyone the thumbs up. Texas rubbed her face, sore but no blood, and looked everyone over. "Come, dear." Mother Superior said again.

As they walked back in, Texas turned to see Bob and Felicity standing by the fire, staring at her. Texas was escorted to another dormitory and sat on the bed as Michael, Raphæl, and Gabreal stood outside playing paper, rock, scissors.

She didn't sleep.

Everyone stood outside of the main entrance, Felicity at attention off to the side, as Bob drove up a beaten-up hatchback the nunnery had hidden in the back. Raphæl and Michæl continued playing paper, rock, scissors while Fred and Texas gave each other a look of disappointment. Bob stepped out "There." He said and sulked off the corner.

Felicity walked up. “He can’t go with you because we have to wait to hear back from Bishop Illios.”

“Suit yourself.” Raphæl said, “Come.” He said to Michael. “No, I’m the leader!” Michæl stiffened. “I say come.” Raphæl reiterated.

“And off!” Gabreal said, spreading his wings as light came out, and the sounds of children singing echoed from the sky.

“I’m the leader!” Michæl said as herm opened his wings, and he too flew off with Raphæl close in tail.

Everyone watched “They’re like children.” Texas said. “Fred, we should go.”

“Are you sure we can take the car?” Fred asked.

“Yes, of course.” Mother Superior said, handing him the keys. Bob interjected, “It’s a dangerous world out there.” And Texas was reminded of her mother’s words.

Texas smiled and hopped in the passenger seat of a rusty, half-working hatchback. Fred waved, and the hatchback sputtered away, kicking soot and dust up, making its way back down the forested pine road that led to the highway.

“So, what do we do now?” Felicity asked.

“We stop her.” Bob said quietly, walking away. Felicity closed on his heel. “Why don’t we just stop her here?” Felicity grabbed his shoulders.

“We can’t do it in front of the nuns. Felicity, you are now a part of the inquisition. Our primary mission is to stop questions.”

Felicity smiled and stood up straight, letting out a muffled yelp of excitement. “We need to call the bishop and take the key.” Bob said, pulling out a phone.

Sheriff Plain had been enjoying his coffee, watching the clouds meander across a blue sky, contemplating the blue, when he saw two large birds flying and make a noticeable dive toward the ground. He promptly stood up and walked the other way, knowing that with these types of issues, you have to do the opposite of what is needed. “Not good. Nope, not good.” He muttered to himself.

They had arrived in less time than a thought and landed by the gazebo, and the Sheriff ran up, his feet growing visibly heavier and slower with each footfall closer to the angels. “You can’t be here. We can’t lose any more houses.”

"Pardon?" Michæl spread his wings again, and the sounds of children singing echoed from the sky.

"Oh, I destroyed a house last time I was here. Come, we have to find Gabby; we lost him on the second star to the right." Raphæl said. "I bet there is an ice cream parlor around here." Herm mused.

"Now, no offense." Staring at the wings. "I understand you chicken men, women-" Sheriff Plain began.

But there was a sound that seemed to reverberate off the sky, the flat expanses of earth that was Nowhere, ND quaked, and everyone's ears bled a little as a sour A note flew across every molecule in the sky.

"Is that!?" Michæl asked.

"It is! Excuse me, ugly man. We have a friend to find!" Raphæl shouted.

"Me? I'm not really ugly?" Sheriff Plain stuttered.

"No, you're pretty ugly." Raphæl added before they both walked off down Main Street.

"Well..." Sheriff Plain hung his head and walked back to his coffee.

Gabriel was sitting on what remained of Mary's front porch, fingering his trumpet, when a light, kind, and sweet, lovingly embraced him. "Gabby!" Two voices shouted in a song-like tone, trying to harmonize with one another. Raphæl and Michael, wings spread, a cacophony of playground enthusiasm, running with fervor and excitement, arms flailing, "Gabby!" They shouted again.

Gabriel stood, spread herm wings, and ran up, embracing them with such a force of wing clasping that it rained in Newark, New Jersey, rather than Central Park.

"We thought we lost you. We stopped here thinking..." Michael said.

"I got sad." Gabby said. "I needed to come back."

"I knew it. And I thought of Ice Cream for a reason." Raphæl said. "Come."

The Frozen Cone was a quiet place, sans the three angels trying to harmonize middle C. "You are too pitchy," Michæl said to Raphæl.

"I am not; you are singing flat." Raphæl said.

"Herms, it just won't work. Not without the music maker." Gabby put his head down. "I don't think he was right to lock himself away. I don't... I'm questioning, for the first time." And with that, Gabby walked to the door.

Michæl and Raphæl looked at one another, "We have decided to interfere." Raphæl said.

Gabby stopped and stared at herm. "The peace will be broken. Which means we'll have to fight."

Michael rose up and puffed out herm's chest. "That means I need to find my sword. We will be going to battle soon!"

"Quick, the ice cream is melting." Raphæl said licking herm cone.

Texas and Fred walked into the Shaky Hand Coffeery. "Fred!" Mpta said, running from behind the counter. "Chima! Your boy is home." And she threw her arms around him.

"Mom." Fred hugged her back.

"Where were you!? The Rhodes house was destroyed; we searched and did–" Mpta saw Texas and brought her in for the hug. "I'm so glad to see you were okay. Mr. Plain said it would be okay, that he talked to you and–" She started crying. "Oh, it's so good to have you home."

A burly man from the back came out, shoulders broad and arms outstretched. "Fred we were worried about you! The Rhodes house is no more, and no one has seen-he looked at Texas. "Oh, Texas!" He wrapped his arms around the three. "I think you should stay here tonight. It's not safe. There has been this woman walking around blowing a horn, saying that the world is ending."

"That's Gabby. Herm's okay." She pushed her head free from his arms. "We are looking for a man with wooden teeth." Texas said.

They all loosened their grip. Chima thought for a moment, and Mpta looked at her. "Do you mean Mr. Washington? He's here every morning at–" And Mr. Washington opened the door.

"You!" Texas yelled, "I need to know more about this key!"

Washington turned and started to walk back out. "Wait!" Texas grabbed his arm, and the dust from his wig peppered her hand.

"Don't touch the customers." Mpta reminded her.

"Please, Mr. Washington, I need to know more about this key." Washington stopped, took a breath, and said, "Have they come for it yet?"

"Who?" Texas stared directly at him.

Mr. Washington took a breath and let out a sigh. "Let's have some coffee."

Mpta brought over a cup of coffee to Mr. Washington, and Texas gently put down the mugs with her wizened hands and turned them so the handles faced their respective customers. She lingered as they stared first at each other, then at her, and then... "I would like to talk to Mr. Washington alone." Texas said.

Mpta, smiled, "Anything for our customers." She turned and walked back to the counter, turning slightly as Chima made his way from the back with another two cups of coffee. Chima jaunted to the table and put down the coffees in front of Mr. Washington and Texas next to the ones from Mpta. "You know," he began. "Mr. Washington, you have been a great customer, but Texas is special, and you should tell her what she needs to know." And Chima stood there waiting for a response that never came until, "Thank you, Chima." Mr. Washington said.

When they were once again alone, Mr. Washington took off his powdered wig and blue frock before taking a sip of coffee. "What do you know?" Washington started.

"Well, I don't know anything. I was told this can open the door to the closet that God locked himself in." Texas began.

Washington nodded in thought. "I heard that too."

"What did you do with your key?" Texas asked.

"I started something. Has an angel come to meet you?" He took a long draft of his coffee.

"Yes!" Texas exclaimed. "I don't like them."

"Them? I only had one. Strange. Did yours pierce the vale?"

"What's that?"

Washington nodded his head and stood up. "I can't help you." He hesitated, shaking his head back and forth. "I just can't."

"Don't go! I have angels and titans and priests and everyone looking for me to do something with it, and I'm here, I'm, I don't know anything about it! I lost my mother over this! I lost my mother, I..."

Washington took a breath and leaned heavily on the table as he offered Texas his hand. "There is a place that might have some answers."

Washington took them to an old building in town with crumbling corners and missing stones. The doors were weathered and scraped as if people were once fighting their way in. The red roof was falling in on itself, and the parking lot had four older cars that were in the same shape as the building: all with square and compasses on the back. Washington hobbled inside and held the door for Fred and Texas, and was hit with the smell of the basement. It was a musk of age and public facilities that had everything from asbestos to black mold hanging in the air.

"I don't really think this is a place for us." Texas said.

"Well, not for you." Washington explained. "Women aren't allowed in our meetings."

"This isn't the Middle Ages." Texas reiterated.

"You don't understand what we do here; it's secret and is not meant for women." Washington said.

Fred piped up, "But I can come in, right?"

"Of course, we're always looking for new members."

"This is stupid." Texas said, She put her hair up in a bun, 'Fred, give me your undershirt." "What?" Despite his questions, Fred took off his shirt and handed Texas the white cotton tee.

She stuffed it under her shirt and maneuvered it to look like a badly shaped belly, making her breasts and stuffed tee gut as one element. "My name is Ryan. Got it?" Washington took a breath and shook his head.

"No, no. They'd never believe you and Ryan is too modern a name for these people; it will raise suspicion." Washington took a breath, "Just follow me." Texas handed Fred back his shirt, and he put it on. Washington pushed the two through the front door past an old dining hall and in through an ornate single open-door frame, where they were met by an equally old man sitting in a chair asleep.

"He's the Tyler, I'll go in. Wait here." Washington said. The door slammed behind him, waking the gentleman.

Texas and Fred looked at one another. Fred nodded his head, "Hello Tyler." The older man smiled and started to nod off again.

Washington came right out. "He's out back."

Around the building, the three heard the chinking sounds of metal on marble and the grunt of a man lifting a hundred-pound boulder. He was strong, with bulging muscles and a spine that looked like it had been compressed over years of lifting. He dropped the boulder on a pile of other rocks and slowly walked back to the previous pile.

"Prometheus." Washington said.

The strong man stopped and looked over, then leaned down to pick another rock and walk it over to the second pile. He saw the group and said, "Washington." In a stoic tone.

"I have someone you should meet." Washington was asking as if his hat was in his hand. "She has a key like me."

And he dropped his boulder. An eagle cried out, and the man instinctively ducked.

The four of them sat at a table that wobbled slightly on the upper floor of an old bar, sipping water, waiting for food to come. Prometheus was tapping a ring that had a series of symbols, from an iron cross to a rose, adorning every inch of its silver surface. Washington was wiping his brow, taking large gulps of water, waiting for Adam's answer.

"When I had a key-" Washington asked.

"You wasted it." Prometheus interrupted. "Texas, right? You have to open the closet. That is the only way out of this."

"The closet? So, it's true. I was told a story of how God locked himself in a closet."

"No." Washington started. "The key can do so much more."

"Washington. Stop." Prometheus started in.

"She has to know. The key can open anything, it can start anything. But, you must pierce the vale..."

"Why didn't you open the closet, Washington?" Fred interjected.

"I started this nation. I started the United States of America with my key." Washington said and Prometheus stood up. "And you wasted it. Washington, you wasted it." Prometheus explained. This time, Washington stood up, "How dare you!" He rolled up his sleeves and put his fists up.

"Come on." He taunted Prometheus.

Prometheus kicked Washington's knee, and the old man dropped. "It is a nation; it is a government. I'm talking about eternity, beyond borders. Beyond Washington. When will everyone stop drawing imaginary lines around themselves? You could have opened the closet, and we'd have Eden again. It would be put back the way it was. Texas, you have to understand. I have helped thousands of key holders throughout the years, and everyone has failed; they have been turned, died along the way, or gone and done something they shouldn't have." Prometheus was on his feet, supporting the weight of his body with his fists on the table as he leaned over Texas.

Washington sat back down and looked outside to see two eagles staring in.

"A lot of people have had it. Arthur, Jesus, Joan D'ace, this guy Jeff, and there was Zhang, and... and, oh, who else? I don't know a lot, but no one person has ever made it all the way to the closet. Most get stopped along the way, some give up, some find a happy spot and try to keep it. But they all forget that there is no stopping, no way to preserve a moment, it is, whether you like it or not, always moving. Now, you have a choice. Would you like to use your key and open the closet?"

"I am not ready for this. I just want to put things back the way they were." Texas backed down.

"I'll take that as a yes! We will have to find the closet again, though." Prometheus stopped and muttered to himself. Nodding a little bit before saying, "The Earth has changed since then. Where to start?" He started pacing before stopping and looking at Texas, "We will save eternity, Texas." Shaking his head, Prometheus reiterated his feelings.

"I don't want this grand epic quest. I just want things back the way they were before I got the key. It was easy, then." Texas said, holding her hand up to calm Prometheus down.

The waitress brought over their food with a smile, and as they all sat back down.

Prometheus said, "Then you're a fool–"

Please Pay Attention

"Hello, my name is Ted, and I'm the villain of the story.
I like murder, and I do have a plan. It's not as if I'm a psychopath,
and I do have a guiding philosophy. You see, we are all on our own.
We are here to exploit others; they are our fuel,
and meaningless outside of their utility."
I'm sorry, I'm supposed to be in the next book. Ted thoughts were left here.

[Ted]

As I was saying:

Fred and Texas were waiting at the entrance of the tavern across from the crumbling building as Washington and Prometheus used the bathroom. "So, you think this guy is for real?" Fred asked.

"I don't know. I don't get a good feeling about this, Fred." Texas started. "I've pushed around since the start. I think-" She stopped as the TV caught her attention.

"And in other news," the talking head on the TV started, "the Dow has plummeted..."

The TV cut to a video of the Federal Reserve chair and some officials from the government. "We have suspended trading today..." Behind the chair was Astarte, dressed in white, golden locks turned up to a bun, smiling. "That's her! That's the woman I saw at the Hellfire club!" Fred said. He turned to Texas. "The sex club..."

Prometheus and Washington stepped out of the bathroom. Washington watched for a moment, noting Texas and Fred entranced. "What is going on?"

"She, the woman in blond. She is a Titan. I know her." Fred said and reached his hand up to high-five Texas. "I knew something about this, Texas."

Prometheus shook his head in agreement. "That is my sister, Astarte." Fred and Texas looked at him. "This is a bit of a family war," He paused and looked at them, "but I am on your side." He said, lightly smiling.

They watched on as the talking head continued to explain, "There were several riots in Chicago, New York-"

"They have already started. This is the way the great turns start. First, they will crash the economy, make people desperate, but before they turn on each other, the nations will turn on nations to distract and blame each other for their own misfortune. I have to go back to the lodge," Washington exclaimed, "there are still people who will help."

"We have to go to California. We have to slow the Titan's progress." Prometheus said and grabbed Texas's hand.

"Whoa!" Texas said, trying to wrench her arm free, but his clasp held, and he stopped.

"We have to go," Prometheus said as Fred leaned in and grasped Prometheus's hand. "Let her go!" Fred pulled as Texas demanded. "Don't touch me."

Washington walked over and placed his hands all around. "Prometheus." He said slowly. Prometheus, let go. "Texas, we have to stop this. They are making a distraction-"

"California, we have to go." Prometheus reiterated.

"How?" Texas began.

"Follow us." Washington led the way, as Prometheus took a step back and held his hand to let Texas and Fred through. They crossed the street to the old dilapidated building and walked below the square and compass that hung over the main entrance. They walked to the back of the building, in a door to the right, and down the stairs. The basement walls were lined with wood planking that hadn't been updated for at least 60 years and ten tables that were evenly spaced, each wrapped with folding chairs. They walked over to the far wall with another square and compass hanging on the wall, this one with a G in the center. Washington pressed the single dot in the middle of the G, and a door popped open, concealed in the wall.

Washington waved everyone over, and as he walked in, he hit a large switch that lit the G in all the square and compasses in all the old Freemason buildings all over the country.

"Texas, Fred, I need you both to come with us. They will be after you now, and we are the only ones who can protect you." Washington stood to the side.

Prometheus led the way. "Follow me." He said, walking through the hidden door and down to the spiral staircase.

Texas looked at Fred, as Prometheus looked back. "Are you taking us to the closet, Prometheus?" Texas said.

Prometheus ignored her and made their way down to a subway long platform covered in cobwebs and an inch or so of soot. Before them stood an antiquated train, dark red in hue, with bits of rust in the corner. Prometheus walked to the front and pounded on the door. An older man opened the door; this one had a long beard, his suspenders held up gray overalls, and a blue and white striped shirt. They whispered animatedly before the conductor pulled out a map.

"Where are we!?" Fred asked.

Texas looked around. "I don't know."

Washington butted in, "We're in a subway station." In the distance, Prometheus turned back to them, making his way to the first car. He lightly leaned his shoulder into the door and popped it open. Washington continued, "We have tunnels crisscrossing the country. Come on, this will take us to our next stop. You should see the private Astor station under Second Street in New York City."

"Are you taking us to the closet?" Texas asked again.

"No, first we must gather our forces, then we will find the closet." Prometheus said, ushering them in.

Close to the same time.

The three angels walked through the aisle of a big store shaped like a box. "They are harder to find than I thought." Gabrielle said, picking up a plastic sword from the aisle and swinging it around. "This won't really hold up."

"I know, but what choice do we have? When was the last time you two were in a store?" Michæl lifted up a piece of plastic armor from the shelf. "I haven't been in one for twenty-four hundred years. When I needed those beans for the cow, then there was that goose... Are these the only weapons we can find?"

"What of guns?" Raphæl asked. They looked at each other and laughed. "No, of course, swords are much more effective. The last time I was at a store was when the woman, Helen, had her key and started that war. Just decimated Ba, I mean Anatolia, I think it's Turkey now. But maybe I'm just hungry. I just can't keep up with how fast the world moves sometimes."

They walked up and down the costume aisle, trying on pirate swords, Roman swords, and medieval swords. "What ever happened to the angel armory?" Gabrielle asked.

Back to the Train.

The train sped through the tunnel, its square and compass emblazoned on the top of the car's ceiling, which was different as it was flanked by two bees. Fred and Texas sank into their plush seats, and Washington paced back and forth. Prometheus walked in from the front car. "It's night right? We have to stop at the terminal hub under the Denver Airport, where they will connect our car to a new engine, but then we will be back on our way."

"So, you have underground trains that just go across the country?" Fred asked.

"Of course, this one is one of the Freemasons, but they work with other groups that need quick and quiet transportation across the US. In case of a devastating attack- this is a lot safer than planes." Washington began.

"What's with the bees?" Fred asked.

"Ah, yes." Washington began. "They spread the pollen that allows fruit and vegetables to blossom. When I started this country, I was that bee."

"Yes, that is obvious." Fred signed.

"There are two philosophies that guide humanity. Only two. Everything else is a derivation of that. I like to call it the bee and the fly. When you see a bee, it is indicative of flowers, fruit, and vegetables. When you find their home, if you choose to follow them, they will let you have their honey. But if you cross them or threaten their queen, their source of power, they will kill. Bees are scary and wonderful; they make things grow and are an indicator of life. They have a collective mind, like an ant; they work as one to make the hive better and will sacrifice themselves to protect the queen.

The fly is a sign of pestilence and plague. They live off of death, and if you follow them home, you will only find decay. They work only for themselves, they work only to find food, and often it is covered in feces; they are attached to the smell of rank and foul orders. The masons are the bees. We have to ready our stingers." Washington concluded puffing out his chest.

"So, bees vs flies?" Fred said. "This isn't very epic."

"Bees vs flies is the greatest of the fights! It's more important than any nation or war." Washington reiterated.

The train edged out of the tail of a mountain range and into the clearing, where it passed into an opening of a wooded glade, where it gently eased to a stop. Prometheus leaped from his chair and ran off, saying, "We're late" he said under his breath. Washington ushered Texas and Fred from the railcar. They gingerly took steps from the door and onto a metal stair that jutted out from the train.

In the distance, Prometheus was briskly walking to a patch of earth that could be seen with a large collection of cars that ranged the entire spectrum of the rainbow. Texas and Fred surveyed the land.

"What is it?" Texas asked.

"It's another secret society. We're gathering all the societies." Washington explained.

"How many are there?" Fred asked.

"Dozens, hundreds. All are trying to find the mystery of the world, trying to understand themselves and who they are. Most are looking for power, trading for better jobs, trying to get in the club, make new connections, whatever. Did you know Walter Cronkite was a part of this one?" Washington marveled.

"I don't know who that is." Fred said.

Washington let out a long sigh. "Prometheus has a plan."

The four of them walked up the long path that wound around a clearing and patches and eventually passed several old camp buildings with large stone chimneys and rows of tents. The path crested to a point that overlooked a pond with a statue of an owl with onyx eyes and a throng of people already gathered, Prometheus stood upon a large rock. He lifted his arms, and they listened as inaudible muffled sounds came from the crowd.

An eagle cawed, and Prometheus ducked instinctively. "Damn birds." He muttered.

"Come on!" Texas said, picking up speed and running to the group with Fred and Washington in tow. Everyone was now in small groups talking while Prometheus stood with a tall man with six fingers named Valentine, who spoke to him in an unknown language. Texas and Fred kept their heads down when Fred bumped into an older woman in white. "Hello dear, you're very young to be here." The woman said.

"Oh, well, I was brought here against my will." Texas blurted out immediately, regretting it.

"Yes, most women were." She smiled. "That is why we have to stick together. Get the rest free, you know. So, to which family do you belong?" Texas paused. "You know, the 'families.' What industry is your family in?" She reiterated.

"I don't know..." Texas said.

"Oh, we're really rich." Fred jumped in. "We have businesses."

"Ah," the woman said. "It's okay to be poor. Most don't think it, but it's not a moral failing. Don't worry, honey, most of us who come from money really shouldn't have any." She said dreamily. "We are scrambling to keep our power and jockey against one another, see who is rich and who isn't, but later you realize that it's all just a silly game." She leaned over to Fred and whispered. "You should never be ashamed about being poor or proud to be rich. But people don't understand that."

There was a cloud clang and Prometheus started. "People, listen to me! There isn't much time!" Everyone quieted down. "There are people coming, and we don't have time for introductions. You all answered the call of the wheel within a wheel, but now I would like to tell you why I called you all here. The Titans are in the open. And," He dramatically paused. There was a quiet laugh, but he continued, "You know of whom I speak; we may call them different names, but we all know of them."

And a voice from back shouted. "It is true."

Prometheus began again. "The Titans have come back, and the economy is crashing. They are doing it again. We will not let this one go under the waves like the last one. The three rings must not sink!" Everyone stared at him. "Say with me. The three rings must not sink." He said again. There was silence.

"Then let us move to Canada, where we can raise an army and start~" A person shouted from back.

"No, we need to fight now!" Prometheus shouted.

"South America is rich with resources; we can move there~" another spoke.

“We’re too old. We can’t fight then now.” Another voice croaked.

The murmurs grew louder, and the crowd was starting to disperse. Washington made his way to the front as the people started to grow in confusion and whispered in Prometheus’s ear.

“Let’s give up!” Someone shouted.

No one was listening. Washington grabbed Texas and brought her up. “She is a key holder!” He said.

Texas held herself up and looked on at the crowd that had now stopped. “Show them the key!” Washington whispered. She lifted the key that was still tied to the leather strip around her neck. It was as if the air stood still, bees hung in mid-flight, a bird beat its wings, and everything slowed down. Texas looked up, and from her hand she fell silence, a force sucking the air and the sounds, emanating and eating light, dimming the world, and rippling out as if she were a stone hitting the stillness of reality. The angles of the incident equaled the angles of reflection, and the reverberations gathered the particles of time, for a moment, which was the center. The center of it all.

“Give me the key!” Someone shouted.

“Give me the key!” Another person shouted. And so, to that, reverberated a clamor as people rushed forward in a cacophony of panic and greed. Texas was to be drowned by a tsunami of hands crashing in waves and swallowing her. But a ring was cast upon the sea, and everyone turned to see where the rope to the lifebuoy had come from, metaphorically speaking, of course.

Rounded to the back, on a hill that had not been there a moment ago, rising from the depths, there, a man stood in a red robe with a staff adorned with a golden cross on it. “I am Bishop Illios. You must not open the closet!” And from behind him, a hundred brightly uniformed men carrying guns brought their muskets to bear.

“We are the inquisition.” A voice said as Bob and Felicity crested the hill, dressed as members of the cloth. “Only we can ask the questions!” He said, holding his sword high, its blade dull now and shorter than before.

Texas turned to Washington. “What’s going on?”

“I don’t know.” Washington started moving forward with his hands outstretched, pushing Fred and Texas back. “The Catholics were not here last time.”

There was a pop followed by what sounded like sharp fireworks until there was a hail of gunfire peppering the crowd. "This is a trap. We need to leave now." Washington said. "Now!"

Fred looked around. "I don't know where we are."

Prometheus grabbed Texas's hand and yelled, "Back at the camps, the cars." As they made their way South.

They froze as a whirling sound from overhead grew, and a rope descended in front of them. A third group of interested parties was showing up. Texas and Fred turned back to the field to see helicopters landing and SUVs driving in, stopping mid-field as men and women came barreling out in black garbs that aimed their guns at both the Bishop's men and the crowd at large.

"I think it's too late." Fred screamed to Texas.

Texas grabbed Fred's hand. "RUN!" Prometheus let go as a soldier descended from the rope, kicking him in the face. They were all separated.

The helicopters were circling the grove, and the government agents dropped from above.

Arresting everyone. "Stay where you are." A voice bellowed from a loudspeaker above. "Do not move." Texas looked up to see Atlas hanging from a helicopter.

And then there was a loud, forced beep, as one of the helicopters spiraled from the sky. From the woods, a small tree was launched, almost clipping the rotors of a Blackhawk. It was Uranus who was working his way through bullets and fists, hacking and crushing anyone and anything that came into his path.

Texas looked back and, among the Swiss guard, she saw Bob high on the hill with a nun next to him.

Texas ran into the woods, Fred reaching for her, but was pushed out of the way by a small cadre of men and women running for their lives. Prometheus ran up beside Texas, "You need to get away alone!" Eagles descended upon him, clawing at his face and pecking at his lower abdomen. He looked over at Fred, who was being carried away in the panic. "Fred!" Prometheus yelled. "Disperse, give them as many people as possible to chase as you can!"

Chapter Nineteen

"Who looks outside, dreams; who looks inside, awakes"

[Carl Jung]

It started as a trickle, as if it were beginning to rain, as the first drop ran down his arm when he came back to his senses. Uranus kneeled upon the ground, a random person's arm in one hand and blood-soaked fingers in the other. He emptied his hand and ran his nails through the dirt and wet earth. Everyone had fled to leave behind burnt-out cars, one crashed helicopter, and a crumbling statue of an old man who looked wild in nature.

Casing from the bullets strewn on the ground, a few lances, and nameless people from the various army groups. Most of the elderly members of the wheel within a wheel had made an escape.

Uranus stretched his neck and looked up to see the ghostly figure of Thomas, who was tied to a tree with his silver thread. Thomas tried to run his hand through the grass he sat upon.

"I think you won," Thomas said.

"It was never about winning," Uranus said.

"This is the most you have talked to me since... Hey, I have a thought. Why am I not flying away or falling through the ground?"

"You don't want to."

Thomas shook his head and tried to touch the grass again. "Then why can't I touch the grass?"

"It's all in your mind. You do what you want." Uranus stopped and looked very serious at Thomas. "It has always been in your mind. Everything."

"I want to touch the grass again. I want to live again. I believe that, why can't I?"

Uranus started arranging the body parts on the grass in the sign of an X, with one stance pointing north and aligning each to the cardinal directions. "This is a shared dream. For you to live again, others and you would have to dream the same dream." Uranus waited. The skies were clear, and the wind rode the air slowly. Uranus pounded his fist against the ground. "We need more."

"More what?"

"More dead. She won't come without the dead." Uranus said.

And Thomas had a thought about life. One he couldn't articulate or understand, and a flash of light came across him. He wasn't where he was, the tether was no more, and he saw a torrent of tornadoes of air that sparkled as static electricity pulsed. For a moment, he saw what looked like a cloth sheet in front of him, as if everything in the world was painted on a large curtain that hung from some impossible rod. It fluttered in the breeze, and a corner curled up. Thomas bent down to look and saw that it revealed a wheel within wheels of gears and pulleys that pulsed with electricity. Then he was back, the tether that was around his neck fell gently to the ground, and was scooped up and thrown by the wind.

He was free.

Texas was running through the redwoods and dense deciduous forest that seemed to loom over her and block her path. Two people, shouting in an indiscriminate tone, brandishing halfcocked ancient guns and long halberds, were on her trail, but outside of the faint echo of a radio call, she didn't know how far back. Texas felt the heat in her lungs constrict her breathing as her legs grew numb, and a second wind took hold of her back, and as a sail she sped forward across the dense landscape.

They screamed, but Texas wouldn't look back. They were howling, and the Doppler of their voices trended red. Their sound rustled in the forest and faded away. She slowed, "Keep going," she said to herself, but ventured a look back. Her foot pinched a tree and fell to the ground.

"Let me help you up." A disembodied voice said. "You need to leave, now."

Texas looked up to see a light blue form and screamed. She wrenched herself away, arching her back like a cat, and crab crawling away as the visage of an elderly priest stood before her.

"Stop screaming!" Thomas pleaded.

Texas shot up and turned, but Thomas was in front of her again with his hands up. "No, please. It's me, Thomas. You watched me die, remember?

"Am I dead?!" Texas panted.

There was a rustle in the woods, and the baying of dogs could be heard in the distance.

Thomas moved close. "Do you have your key?"

Texas scrambled, pawing at her neck and pulling the key from beneath her shirt.

"You need to..." Thomas disappeared, flicking in and out. She watched as the remnant of his face scrunched up. "The key–" his voice echoed off the trees and disappeared on the wind. "The- inquisition- Ask the questions-"

"What do you mean!?" Texas screamed.

A cloaked figure showed up with a clipboard. "I'm looking for..." There were gunshots in the distance, as grunting and the clanking of metal chewed through the air. "It's not your time. I was asked to get you somewhere safe, or it might be your time, I don't know. Either way, come, you need a hug." And the dark enveloped her, its arms were as smoke, and she felt a hollow about her as if the earth were swallowing her from below; a light shone that felt like love and gravity.

And before her was. "Texas!" A voice said. Texas looked up to see ~ "Mom?"

Later

"It's up to us now..." Bob said, screaming over howling wind that skirted around his head. They hit a bump, and another piece of the high-end American car fell off. The top was missing, torn, or cut off from something at the Grove. Felicity sat next to him, trying to tune into an AM radio station as they crossed the California border into Nevada and made their way into the desert.

"We are the inquisition!" She smiled and turned the dials to find a station broadcasting the news and adjusted the volume over the hum of the wind that whipped around her. She leaned out and let her habit fly. "Robert," she began, "we have to find Texas."

Felicity looked at him "They probably have her now. We have to go back and save her. Who were those people?" She paused and looked out onto the road and the bleak landscape that held a barren future. "You think Bishop Ilios is dead?"

"No." He gripped the wheel. "This is what I have prayed for. We are on a quest now!" He looked at her.

"We shouldn't help her open the closet; right, Bob?" Felicity was having doubts as the sand peppered her cheeks.

Bob took a breath and looked out. "No. It is dangerous. The Bishop is right, the church has gone this long without a God, we don't need one now. We are the inquisition. No one can ask the questions besides us."

"But Bob."

"I am the inquisition! I ask the questions. We know there are angels. We know there are these creatures called Titans. We know that everything is falling apart. Felicity, it is up to us to fix this. That is our quest."

"Then what are we going to do?"

"We're going to take the key back." Bob pressed the gas, and the car sputtered. He looked down to see the gas indicator drop from full to empty as all the lights started flashing."

Later.

Washington stood with a portly man outside a giant recycling plant dotted with four large dump trucks in the back.

"This is crazy." Washington's companion said.

"It is, that is why it will work. We cannot sit back." A woman walked up in a large black dress and clutched Washington's hand. "There is no defense with those that we fight now, Franklin. There is only an attack. Now, man up We have to get moving. The other side isn't going to wait."

"Martha, I appreciate that you won us the war–" Franklin began.

A woman in a dark blue blazer stood beside them, writing in a pad. "I hate to interrupt, but we have to move on this. Do you have any questions?"

"Let's see inside." Martha started.

They walked into a cavernous building held up by large circular tumblers that would sort the plastics from the metals. Washington looked over the mechanics and turned to Franklin. "How long can we hold?" Franklin pulled out an abacus. "About three years, the wind has been with us."

Martha started pressing buttons as the tumblers sparked to life. "This is good. Franklin, you can't put a cost on life."

Franklin stood up straight. "Sure, you can."

Far away.

Jackson Hole, Wyoming, holds many secrets, one of which is a long stretch of interwoven tunnels. One of the said tunnels was experiencing a convoy of heavy-load trucks and one SUV entering the facility at a progressively faster pace.

"Mr. Jefferson," A mild man said. "The companies have been ordered to produce at full capacity."

Jefferson shook his head up and down before putting the phone in his hand to his ear. The sound of machines whirling and reverberating on the other end echoed through speaker.

"Martha?" Jefferson began. The mechanics clanked over the phone; Jefferson spoke up. "We have to keep this from turning into a progress trap."

"Jefferson," Martha yelled into the receiver. "Take the gold stores and invest. We are buying the last of the recycling plants. We will make things, sell them, they will be then recycled, and we will take everything apart and sell the parts back to the factory for no profit."

"It doesn't make sense."

"Jefferson. All we have to do is keep people busy. The money will just exchange hands like the products, nothing new, nothing old. We can keep that going for three years."

Jefferson nodded. "It's just so crazy it might work."

Chapter Twenty

"To have life, you must have death."

[Duality Doubles: inventor of the flap that is on leather bags; not credited]

Texas awoke to a flattened land, high with mountain ranges off in the distance, and an arid quality to the air that cracked her lips. The grass beneath her squinched and scrunched with each step while the wind poked at her face with an icy chill. She looked around and yelled, "Hello!"

There was an echo from the valley that confirmed no one was really listening. Or at least not wanting to shout back.

"Hello!" She shouted again, but still no response. "Okay. Okay. Okay." She said to herself. She looked at the sky for helicopters; everything was flooding back. Dream? Dead? She patted her body; it felt solid enough. Her breathing was increasing, her hands shaking, and she shook her head, saying, "Okay, okay, okay." She listened to the birds, the wind, and the grass.

"Get to the closet." She said. There were trees fifty yards forward, and she started to run.

Her ears perked; there was still nothing. As she breached the tree line, her feet crunched beneath pine needles and dead leaves that blanketed the forest floor.

"Hello." Someone said. It was ghostly, as if a wind made manifest.

Texas dropped to the ground and looked around, closing her eyes and listening. No dogs and shouts. There were no sounds of gunfire. It was quiet.

"Hello." The voice again. This time, more panicked. Texas whispered back. "Hello?"

"Hi." Texas fell to the ground and scurried away as the voice was directly behind her, lapping upon her ear. She turned, putting herself against the back of a tree, hands defensively out in front of her.

It was a thin, small figure, with a slight glow about it. Its eyes were wide, curious, with its head tilted slightly and an unnatural smile. "Hello." It said again.

"Are you an angel?" Texas leaned in more.

"I am! I have been lost for some time now. I heard you say hello, and it's been many years. It's so wonderful to meet!"

"Yes" was Texas's response. She sighed and shook her head. "Look." She took a deep breath and started again. "Look, I haven't had the greatest of luck with angels."

"Nonsense! Oh, it's so good to talk to someone again! It's been ages." Herm said.

"I need to get to the closet. Do you know where it is?" Texas tried to think back to before. A moment before, she was there. Someone was there. A little here.

Now.

The angel lit up, herm nearly clapped its hands, but as herm's hand swung closed, there was a vacuum that seemed to absorb the air rather than radiate out. "Oh, yes, I'm very good with directions."

"You do!" Texas leaped forward. "Yes, I said I did, so I do."

Texas waited a minute as the angel stared at her. It started looking around and picked up a leaf.

"So...." Texas began.

"No, I never learned how to sew." Herm said.

"No, I mean so... are we going to go?" Texas begged the question.

"Where?" It kept looking at the leaf. "I love life." Herm said.

"To the closet. We need to go to the closet." Texas reminded Herm.

"Oh, yes!" And with that, the angel spread its wings to the sound of children singing and took off.

"What about me!?" Texas screamed.

The angel landed directly in front of her. "Right!" Grabbed her and flew up again, causing Texas to blackout for a time.

When Texas regained consciousness, she saw the great deserts of Nevada giving way to the flat green land of the Midwest. Her breath was labored, and her head was fuzzy from the thin atmosphere, and she reached out to the angel to muster, "I need more air." The angel looked at her and thought for a moment. There was a pause. It looked at her and back to the flight path again before smiling, realizing what oxygen was, then making a shallow descent.

Texas took an enormous breath. "Where is the closet?" She asked. The Angel looked at her. "Where are we going again?"

Texas looked at herm. "What do you mean!?"

"I mean, I don't know our destination." The angel said.

"The closet. The closet, God hid himself in!" Texas screamed.

"Right, I don't know where that is." The angel nodded.

"What do you mean! You said you knew where it was."

"Oh, then I was mistaken. I must have thought you meant another closet. I'd have to find my brothers to know where that is."

"Put me down!" and immediately regretted saying that as the angel let go. "Pick me up!" She screamed as the angel scooped her up.

"Is this better?" The angel asked.

"Yes. Gently put me on the ground somewhere safe below us. On the ground. Safe." She reiterated.

The angel gently moved to the ground and put her down in front of an old diner with a half-lit sign, two cars parked in front, and stained metal siding. The land was barren around the structure, giving way to an open field and a long stretch of highway that curved at the edge of the earth. "Do you know Gabby?" Texas asked.

"I love Gabby! Herm's by best friend."

"Great, because we need to get a hold of him, herm. Can you do that... I'm sorry, I don't even know what to call you."

"My name is Uriel."

"Uriel, I need to find Gabby. Can you help me do that?"

"Yes!" Uriel said with enthusiasm.

"Not like last time though, like you know where he is and how to get to herm."

"Yes! I mean I will try." Uriel said. "Wait here." And herm ran off down the road.

"You have wings!" Texas shouted.

But herm didn't listen.

Inside the diner, Texas checked her pockets to find some money but only had enough for a coffee and some toast. The old man at the end of the long counter looked over, sneered as the voice on the radio jutted in, "And trading has been suspended as the Dow continues to plummet. In international news, riots continue to spread across India with multiple groups claiming responsibility for terrorist acts. Europe has closed its borders as Russia makes advances into the former Eastern Bloc nations, as the United States pulls out of NATO due to continued domestic conflict."

Texas looks around "Have to open the closet." She said under her breath. "The Republic of Florida has made a petition to secede from the union–" Texas sipped the coffee harder now. There was a shadow on the world now.

"I just want to go home–" Texas said. There was weight upon her, physically, when she felt hands grab under her arms, lift her up, and through the roof and into the sky.

"I found herm!" Herm's voice shouted.

Thank you for coming this far.

Long ago, before time was time, there was a place.

Taurus ruled in the sky and gave way to the Ram when the six twin sons of Atlantis could no longer find that which was the prime mover. To be clear, in the beginning, when all was void, the prime mover would cover an area of space before moving 90 degrees to its edge, and once again finding the circumference of its knowledge, before moving 1/6 the circumference of a circle and finding once again its limit.

It started slowly. No one knew at first; most just felt like something had changed, that there was something that was once there that wasn't there anymore. It wasn't until a year later that people started asking: Where's the music?

The angels were the first to realize they could no longer hear the music that had once had been playing so mightily in their heads. And they looked upon the gates to Eden that closed once again. The sons and daughters who had been forgiven and were allowed to gaze upon the tree of life and the tree of knowledge had become overgrown and untended.

The tree of life was no longer cared for but instead allowed to grow many dead branches; its leaves speckled in yellow, its trunk dark and wide, were only cared for by a large bird at the top, that some might call a phoenix or Nicole. The roots stretched forth as a dragon stretches into the earth and touched every land. It is from this tree that all life begins and continues. A single Peach rested upon its branches, waiting to be plucked.

The tree of knowledge that had borne many fruits since then was still overflowing. Those that were allowed back in the garden had gathered around the table and were waiting for their host so that they could partake in honey and wine, and water and mana. They could eat of bread that would fill and nourish, for it is these who were chosen because of their piety to be the emissaries across the globe.

But over the course of 12 meals, they grew more and more despondent with each other, angry over the details. They all agreed that they should love one another, they all agreed that humans have a right to exist, and that they are the cultivators and stewards of the land. But as the night progressed, the idea that all should live turned into a discussion of, "Well, not the jerks. Right, jerks should be allowed to live." And then from "Well, not the jerks" went to "Well only the people who are smart enough to farm." And then to "Not only do they have to be smart enough to farm, but they also have to be smart enough to invent." And so on and so on until there was a fight that only 12 individuals out of all 10 million should exist. So, it came that we should love all, for we should love all, except the people that upset us, or the people that were rude, or the people that didn't deserve it, the people that stole our fruit, the people that made imperfect pies, and so on.

And thus, they bickered, and every time the Prime Mover tried to steer them back to the basic principles of love, charity, and hope, it would remind them that hope for a better day means there would have to be bad days, and that's okay. If only good things would happen, humans would never have an understanding of what a good thing is, for they would have nothing to compare it to. And as such, the idea of hope meant you had to have despair, and charity meant that you had to have inequity; you could not have one without the other, and love meant that you also had to have hate. All three virtues required their opposite for them to exist. That is where the fight began, and so by the end of the night, their host, who set a table before them of good and plenty, decided that it was time they retired, and they gave them a moment amongst their thoughts. They let themselves into the closet and locked it from the inside. When all those around the table realized what had happened, there was panic.

The cherubs, Yael and Jael, came in and escorted everyone out, saying, 'thank you for coming' and giving them parting gifts of cured meat, unleavened bread, and fruit that they grew. Yael and Jael said, "it was time to think about what they did and where to go next."

As the last of the humans, a couple named Prometheus and Eve, were cast out of the garden, on the other side of the globe, a small shepherd tended to a flock of sheep that was gazing into a stream and asked What's the point of this before throwing up a key.

The Oera linda, a book of some renown, states:

"And the herms looked upon the earth, and below the seas they gave a shudder, and the Titans decided to look upon the heavens. But knowing their eyes weak they gathered all the men and people of the earth and created a monument that would stretch forth. It started low as that of a hill and grew out in breadth and depth until it covered most of Sunderland and then rose up higher than any form the earth had made. From there the people of earth would trek to its apex and look upon the land for its creator. They would look at the sky for their mover. But all for not. For that which began all could not be found and so they continue to build.

Those that the creator made to guide humanity, both the strong and willful as well as the innocent and young, took part in this endeavor. And so, it rose and grew in such a state that those that dwelt upon it were known as those that lived in the city. It was a time that drew all manner of people to it, even those within the three-ring city that sat on the edge of what is now Alkebulan.

When the last person reached the summit, the tower to peer once more into the heavens and lay a stone, it was lost and collapsed. And the summit that was once an instrument of discovery came apart and the city and the tower fell into itself, it's mass causing a cascade of earth and soil into the ocean and into the sky with a clatter and clang, and brush that it blotted out the sun for three days and caused a wave that traversed around the globe reclaiming parts of the land back into the sea.

It was known that the one who created it had hidden themselves away, knowing that if a child were to be directed by their parents all their lives, that the child would never learn themselves to be the parents of the subsequent generation."

Yeal and Jeal sat on an old brick wall layered with two rows of brown clay brick and filled with rubble from walls that didn't work. It was a place called the city of Babillim. There was a red hue casting itself upon the sky, and all the animals were out, let free to twilight's air. The summer was drawing to a close, and as the night became cool, the wind would be drawn into the town, kicking up sand into torrents flying as if birds in the sky. A few granules pecked at the skin that encased the luminescent figure who was shuffling herm feet.

"Lovely, I never knew humans could run as fast as they do." Yeal said.

Jeal smiled, "When properly motivated, they do very well indeed." The tower had fallen.

The flames drowned out the screams of people no longer able to converse with one another as they darted to the left and the right, thinking that that movement would somehow help them say, "Help me! My house is on fire, and I don't know what to do!"

Jael took out herm's flaming sword. "Welp, they're not getting in here."

"I would say not." Yael agreed, equally as luminescent, sitting beside and watching the city burn. "Oh, look there." Herm said, "that young man has the right idea." They looked on as a boy took the sheep from a pen and scattered them to the hillside, running after them with his two dogs.

"And look down there." The angel said to a group of people, watching the city burn as people tried to bring all manner of water to quench the fire or smother it with sand wherever they could. A group of 13 people yelled things like "What do we do?", "Help me!", "I think I've gone blind!", "I'm in charge now!" As they sat upon the wall, the two beings looked behind themselves to see a large expanse of land that was shielded from the sand and wind and all manner of destructive forces that they were protecting for no apparent reason. "So, what do we do now?" Asked the first angel.

"We still have the trees to protect. And what of the humans running around? Well, they'll go back with their kind, I guess." The second angel said.

And those that survived did just that. Jael and Yeal touched fingers, and the veil was pierced.

We Should Be More Traditional

"It's a place and a title. Please note below."

[Nowhere, ND]

Texas and Uriel landed in front of the shambles of a house that occupied the middle of Westgate Road, with the numbers thirty-three swaying with a slight breeze from left to right. Uriel looked around, "I don't see Gabby." Texas stopped and stared. "I'll go find herm." Uriel said before, once again taking to the sky, leaving Texas alone.

Texas forgot, though seemly impossible, she had been distracted to such a degree by her house, her mother's house... yes, even her mother was still there–in her mind at least. They were here, and Mary was in the kitchen cooking, and when Texas came home, she'd be there.

They would sit on the couch and watch TV, and they would sit across from one another at the dinner table and laugh and argue.

Mary's face came back. Texas couldn't remember it before, but now, in the specific moments, she saw Mary's eyes, crow's feet patted around the edges, and smile lines that crossed her cheeks. It was never the big things, but the little, a laugh and a smile. The awkward talks or the moments of heated exchange, but it was the feeling that lingered, not the specifics. The feeling of Love. She dropped down to her knees and cried. Texas couldn't stop the tears from filling the ground as she stumbled to catch her breath, and her pinky shook as she clenched her fist.

The screech of a tire and a car door opening from behind her stopped the emotional outburst. Texas heard the words, "You left me! Why didn't you come back!? I'm sick of this! I've tried over and over again to show you how much I love you. I have done everything to show you how much I care, and you just don't care about me. You showed me that everything that I do doesn't matter, and you have been taking advantage of me! You left me!"

Texas turned around to see Fred, and behind him was Asteria, the Titan, with blond curls emerging from a long black Lincoln. "It's not some crush! It has never been. You left me! I followed you through everything, and I was here to help you, and not once did you ever ask me how I was feeling or say thank you for coming with you!"

"Fred." Texas squeaked as she lapped back tears, keeping her face forward and head down, staying still.

"No, it's not about you today, you left me, and it's not about me right now. I mean it is about me, Fred, I... Aren't you listening to me?"

Texas froze and kept her head down. She stilled her breath and closed her eyes.

Fred laughed, turned, and stomped down the street. Muttering and throwing his hands in the air all the way to his house several streets over. Texas didn't have the strength to move anymore; so, instead, she took a seat in the rubble and looked at Asteria. The Titan walked over slowly, watching everything unfold, and asked quietly, "Are the angels around?"

Texas shook her head no.

"I'm glad I found you. I was worried I wouldn't. I found Fred after Atlas's little stunt. You know he was looking for you. Did you look for him?"

Texas shook her head no.

"He was the one who knew you'd come home or at least try. We figured we'd start here and drive our way back. I have six helicopters right now looking for you." Asteria sat next to her.

Texas just sat shaking her head up and down.

"Oh, my poor dear." Asteria cupped Texas close to her and pressed her head against her chest. Texas heard her heart beating, moving from an upbeat to a slow melody, her heart moved to sync, and her breath matched. Texas felt the warmth rising, the pain, fight, all, sad, mad, glad, happy, lost, found, made, unmade, and here her tears found an opening. They streamed down as they were held back by every cell in her body, and she heard the sky open up to mirror her emotions. The world, too, was crying as the water poured from the heavens, and Asteria didn't move; she didn't try to find shelter or think of anything outside of that moment.

"I'm here for you." Asteria said to Texas, and she too started to feel, holding her tight, and for some reason, Asteria cried; she too felt the weight of the moment and let herself be with Texas.

Ten minutes went by, and a red cardinal landed on Texas's shoulder before flying off. "Sometimes you just need a good cry." Asteria said, wiping the rain from her face and the tear from her eyes.

Asteria took a second and looked around. It was quiet; the sun parted the clouds. "Let's have some tea."

They sat at the table in the house, Texas, in her mother's pink chair that somehow migrated from the living room to the kitchen as Asteria sat on a stool. Asteria brought tea with her and boiled a kettle on what was left of the stove before fixing a cup for Texas. "I need you to understand something: you cannot open the closet. Do you know what will happen if you do?"

"It will fix everything." Texas whispered.

"You seem to think that, I don't know. Why do you think that when you open it, it will fix everything? You cannot, you are a small town girl, and I think it would be best if you just stay here." Asteria walked up to the broken windows and the broken holes in the shattered roof and walked inside to see shambles on shambles of a home that Texas once knew. "God abandoned us. You understand that, right? It's just you and me. I can do more than fix everything; I can make it nice; I can do everything here." She lifted up a curtain. "No one will help you. That's not how the world works."

Texas looked around and saw everything; she put her hands in her hair and felt a clenching in her chest as she rubbed her fingers on her scalp.

"I need to show you something," Asteria said, and with that, she put her hands to pray, dropped to her knees, and intoned an E in such a way that the modulation of her voice ran up and down to create a word unknown to Texas that pierced the veil. And there was a shimmer upon the world. Texas looked upon the shimmer, and the world was but a shadow projected on a screen that waffled and waved, being blown by some unknown wind.

Asteria was standing beside Texas, and she grabbed her hands. "Follow me." Asteria reached down and tugged the curtain as if it were hanging from some invisible rod, and pulled back to see an intricacy of wheels upon wheels that moved in a magical machine, perfectly and fluidly, cleanly as a watch that stretched on to Infinity. "Texas, you have to see the workings of the universe. This is not the world that you know, but the world behind the world, the one that makes your world run. It is almost mechanical in nature and yet built out of love. And it is from that love that evil is born, and it's from that evil that is born more love is created, and on it goes. This is the great machine."

Texas flittered her eyes back and forth to find, in the center of each cog, within each wheel, there was a hole for a key. She grasped the key that was around her neck and stretched her hands out. Asteria grabbed her shoulders, and before Texas knew it, the curtain was being pulled once again. And somehow in that place, that wondrous machine, she felt peace and absolution as if things were working in concert, though she could not feel it. The curtain fell back into place. She was back in the world where it was, but once again, chaos. Texas turned to Asteria, "Please open it up again, whatever that was." Asteria looked at her and shook her head, no.

"Everything is in order, Texas. The world is the way it is for a reason, and there is no reason for you to change that. It is best for all if you leave it where it is. Not because I don't want the closet open or because you do, but because humans cannot be changed. Imagine the chaos that would ensue if humanity were told that everything that they hate and everything that they're angry about is actually good and has a purpose. Texas, let us rebuild your house, let us set things right as they can be, but in doing so, you have to remember–"

And Texas looked at her, "But can you bring my mom back?"

And Asteria looked at her, "No, but you can find love again, and no one will tell you the truth like I will. They will give you wishes and promises that there's some great mystery, and some great closet, and some great thing out there that will help you ~ I won't. People will look for the key, they will want it, and they will take it from you. They will find this town; they charge it and take everything. They will burn it down just to find you." Asteria took a breath and held Texas's hand. "I can give you one month without anyone coming into the town." Their eyes met. "And, if you like that, maybe I can give you that protection the rest of your life?" She said.

Texas looked at her, knowing what the deal was... "But, you'll do it for me for the key?"

"Yes!" She smiled and leaned in, holding her shoulder. "I knew you were a smart one." And with Asteria, she made a slight laugh before turning and walking back to her car.

Texas didn't know how long she sat in her broken home, legs folded, and rocking without her mind saying a word, but it was long enough for the light to go down and the moon to rise. Texas felt a heaviness upon her chest as Gabriel arrived more gleeful than ever. "It is so wonderful to see you again, Texas. Do you remember me?" Gabby paused and sat beside her. "I'm Gabby, your guardian Angel. I think I blew my horn for the world feels like it's ending. Isn't it wonderful!"

Texas looked at herm, "I'm going to bed." And with that, she walked upstairs and down the hall to her room that now had cracks on every wall and plaster falling from the corner of the ceiling, as it leaned slightly to the center. She dusted off her bed, lay her head down, and fell asleep.

Deep.

It was the heavy sleep without movement or feeling, where her breath was labored and

The birds started their morning song, and she awoke to what felt like a dream. She could smell eggs being cooked in the kitchen, and for a moment, she forgot where and when she was. Then the cracks appeared. She opened her eyes and saw holes, soot, and there was a smell of burning and melted plastic. Next was the sounds of a mess emanating from downstairs.

She walked gingerly down to the first floor to find Gabby cooking her breakfast. And Texas did something she had never done, she sat down at the table and prayed; prayed for guidance, prayed for help, prayed for the feeling to go away. She didn't really pray to anyone; she didn't evoke some God, or a God; she was trying to get the attention of anything that was listening. Maybe it was just to herself.

There was a knock on the door, and Sheriff Plain was standing on the porch with the townsfolk behind him, including Fred's parents, each one holding a board of wood, some with toolboxes, some with cloth, three with a window. The Sheriff took off his hat and said "Miss Rhodes, we're here to help. We're awfully sorry for everything that you've been going through." And with that, one by one, they shuffled in, taking the broken things and putting them on the lawn to be thrown out. The material, the boards, and the windows lay neatly next to them as they started repairing the gaps and holes and mudding the cracks. Gabby came walking out, "There you all are!" Herm said, bringing out tea and random food, some torn lettuce, several apples, burnt toast, and fresh flowers with mustard on them. Each person buckled their knees as herm walked by, feeling heavy and sick.

CHAPTER 23

"Per my last Chapter, I didn't say you had to like it"

[Felix Von Bruder]

It had been nearly ten days since the last of the town's people left Texas's family home, and Texas hadn't really moved from her bedroom. She hadn't eaten, and while it wasn't a self-imposed fast, she wasn't hungry. People would bring up a glass of water for her every hour and would check in, but she would roll over and pull her blankets up, letting the strands of fire red peak out, while Sheriff Plain would stop in and make sure they weren't making too much noise.

At night, Gabby would come in through the window after she was asleep, bright and chipper, and would sit at the foot of her bed, rubbing her feet and calves while she fell asleep. Texas would say, "Go away, Gabby." But herm never did. Several times, Texas would wake in the middle of the night, and Gabby was just sitting still. Herm would smile and wave, before Texas once again rested her head, but herm was always gone before the sun rose.

The townspeople had made it just the way it was; no nail or trim was out of place from where it originally was. Indeed, the whole of the building, sans a small miscut from the boy down the street, Glavin, you'd never have known it was torn to shreds and cheese-holed. Texas played back in her head what Asteria said, Stay home, don't ask questions, don't look for the closet. Over and over again, she thought through Asteria's words.

There was a heaviness in her chest, and she knew from the weight on her shoulders who was knocking at her door.

"Texas?" The voice said. "It's me, Sheriff Plain. Your friend, the strange one with the dress thing. He." He lowered his voice. "He or she?"

"Herm" a disembodied voice said.

"Stop making things complicated! It is either he or she!" There was a breath. "He is here to take care of you. The house is in tip-top shape, and we each cooked you a dish and put it in the freezer for you. You should be good for a month... if you'd eat." He paused. "I'll come check in on you in three days. Till then, your friend will say he'd be here."

"Close enough." The voice said next to Sheriff Plain.

Texas stirred as the door opened a crack. "It's me, Gabby, your guardian angel. Do you remember me? I'm here to help you."

"Go away, Gabby," Texas said.

"But you must understand I'm here to help."

Texas thought back to the last couple of days. "Where were you then!?" as she turned and sat up.

"I was here." Gabby said.

"Where? You weren't with me when I was being shot at, when the house blew up, when I was at the nunnery, when... You were never there!" She blurted out.

Gabby thought for a moment. "I was at the nunnery."

"And I almost was burned alive!"

"You're right, but I'm here now. I'll bring you some food. Humans love food."

"Just leave!" She said.

The next morning, Gabby had set off the smoke alarm twice and blew his horn, still off tune, once, before Texas made it down the stairs. When she got to the third step, it no longer squeaked, and that made her sad. It was a good squeak, and now it was gone. Gabby was over the stove, like Mary, making eggs, attempting, as the shells were still in the pan. It looked like herm had to test how to break an egg several times as a few sat on the counter, broken and dripping yolk on the floor.

"I remember," Gabby began, "Mary made these. Oh, I miss Mary." Texas couldn't say her name, but shook her head in agreement.

"Here," Gabby brought over the hot pan with the eggs in it and placed it on the unfinished wooden table, almost the same as they had before. "Eat!" Herm said.

"I need a fork." Texas stood up and walked over to the drawer that had the forks, but when she opened it, it had only spoons with a note, 'forks will be delivered in a week,' someone had written. She grabbed a spoon and sat down. The first bite was crunchy, but it woke her up.

Gabby brought over a large pot of tea and sat down with her, pouring them both a cup. "What do you do on a normal day?" Gabby asked.

"What do I do?" Texas reiterated, her tone was level, as exhaustion rested upon her. "I don't know. I guess, on most days." She thought. "I don't know. I just don't know." And she stopped and thought.

"Well, today, I'm going to do nothing. Most days I don't really do anything." Gabby said. "No, most days I walk around and help people, but I don't think I'm really good at it. You know, but I keep practicing at it."

"Gabby," Texas stared at herm. "You're an angel, right?"

"I am! I like answering questions I know about."

"Where is the closet?"

"Oh, I don't know. I don't like answering questions I don't know."

"How do angels not know where the closet is?"

"I'll tell you a secret." And Gabby leaned in very close. "I don't think we know much of anything." And herm took a long draft of herm's tea. "We work off of emotions, not intelligence. There is a lot of panic."

They both sat there in their revelations and nodded at each other. There was a ding from the counter, and they looked over to find a phone plugged in. Texas looked at Gabby, "That's yours?" Texas stood up and turned it over, her face opened up the home page that was a picture of her and her mom. There was a single app, the local bank, that was prominently displayed on the front with a notification on it. She opened it and found a million dollars neatly in her account.

Another ding bounced on the phone; the number preprogrammed by Asteria said For you, honey. It's a dangerous world out there. You should stay home. Texas thought back to her mother and smiled, then the sadness came back and wrapped her in its grief.

Texas was on the road, biking her thoughts to their conclusion. Up and down the streets, an inkling took, and veered right. Up the old road, past the welcome sign, and to the town's edge, and found–

A large group of people gathered. Some gnashed their teeth, weapons bared, some with a star that ate through steel, and others clearly bored. All were armed.

In front of the group were two women, both equally well dressed and calm. One donned in black tight-fitting clothes with a bulletproof vest, a rather large gun, and a balaclava covering her face, the second, unperturbed, in a business suit with a tight bun and heels. The one in the suit stepped forward and identified herself as Asteria's lawyer. She started speaking in tongues like ipso facto, ad hoc, quid pro quo, and so on. The other was a clever person with a dictionary, challenging her on where the town ends and the town begins. They all saw Texas...

The attorney walked over briskly to the town's start, pulling out a piece of chalk, she drew a line, looked Texas in the eye, and said. "For your own good, you shouldn't cross this line. It's dangerous out here."

Chapter 24

"1000 grams of flour, 800 grams of water,
20 grams of salt, and 200 grams of sourdough starter"
[Me]

Later

Texas left Sheriff Plain pacing at the town line. He said there was nothing to fear, but the faces of the crowd said: Yes, there was something to fear.

At home, Texas could hear the clatter of dishes that echoed off the cold walls as she ran her fingers along the spines of Mary's books that they stacked back in the same order and same condition, standing guard over the hallway. The internet hadn't produced any results on the closet; that, or her search strings weren't very advanced. God's Closet – a nightclub in Vancouver, very swank. God's Closet – a gay bar in Soho. The closet that God hid himself away in – a book, the feminine mystic, and so on. She looked at the books every day of her life and had never really read the titles. Hypnerotomachia, The Republic, Excerpts of the Nag Hammadi Library, The Order Linder, The Lost Chapters, Secret Teaching of All Ages, Isis Unveiled, The Secret Doctrine, The Book of Law, and so on. There had to be some mention of the closet. The shelves were too straight now. The old one bowed in the center from years of support.

She had started on the left of Mary's religious section and kept moving her way down, pulling one book at a time and bringing it downstairs to the table to add it to the books she found all throughout the house. There was a sticky smell in the air, and Gabby smiled, opening up the stove to reveal a lasagna in the oven as a squirrel and a chipmunk came in to hand him oven mitts and turn off the stove. "It's a miracle!" Gabby said.

"What in the princess are you doing?" Texas asked.

Gabby stood up straight and lifted herm's hand, beckoning the bird through the window to sing a song. "I made us food! And it's a miracle! Saint Francis used to love to cook with animals, but he always asked to wash their hands. I think I forgot; we may not want to eat this..."

Texas put her hands over the food, "It's still cold."

Gabby dropped the tray and ran into the living room. Texas looked down; it wasn't her family dish. It was something her neighbors brought over. She looked around. The dishes were not hers; in fact, nothing in the house was hers anymore. Her chest felt tight, and from the other room, Uriel came in. "What are you doing here?" Texas screamed.

Uriel pulled a large sword from its sheath, and Texas felt the heat from the flames that emanated from the steel shaft. He held it up high and gently slung it down on a loaf of bread that was lying on the table, licking the lacquer finish. "Would you like a piece?" Herm asked.

"No!" And she shook her head. "What are you doing here?" she asked. There was a crash at the window. They looked over to see Raphæl getting up. Uriel walked over and opened up the glass, checking for damage.

"The window is very clean! I thought it was open. I'll go through the front door." Raphæl said and ran around to the front and into the kitchen.

"What is going on here?" Texas yelled emphatically.

"I was getting toast because Gabby was feeling..." Herm hesitated. "Herm was feeling B.A.D."

There was a gasp from Raphæl. "I know!" Said Uriel. "That hasn't happened since, I can't remember." Herm turned to Texas. "And I'm getting him toast. It's the closest to mana I can find, and..." Herm grabbed the kettle and turned it on. "We're making tea."

The angels retreated to the living room to sit with one another. Texas walked in to see them sitting quietly with one another, touching wings. "Angels don't get sad." She said.

"I can feel, thank you very much. Your sadness has been contagious. And..." Gabby hesitated. "I don't think we actually know anything. We're B.A.D."

"You're not bad." Texas said, her heart sinking a little at the sight of them.

"We are B.A.D." Uriel said. "It's the worst we can be. It means Being A Dunce. Useless."

"What do you mean?" Raphæl asked as his wings vibrated slightly.

"We don't know where the closet is, we don't know how to help, and we don't know how to make lasagna." Gabby continues.

"I made toast!" Uriel reminded them as herm stood up and thrust the uneaten, blackened toast in everyone's face one by one.

"True." Raphæl said. "And we knew how to find each other."

"We did!" Gabby said.

"So, you're better?" Texas asked.

"I think we are!" Uriel said, handing Texas the toast. The whistle of the kettle stirred them, and they all ran to the dining room. "Come have a cupa with us!"

Texas sat down.

The angels grabbed each other's hands and held them tight. "Let us pray," Uriel said. "Dear Texas," She looked up. "We hope that you find love, a family, and food. We pray to Texas..."

"Wait! Please don't pray to me." Texas said.

"Well, everyone keeps saying God is in the closet, so I guess all that is left is you." Uriel said.

"Yeah, yeah," Raphæl and Gabby said in unison. Texas shook her head.

"We're also hungry..." Uriel concluded. Texas stood up, "What would you like?"

"Food!" they all said.

Texas washed her hands in the kitchen and pulled out a plate and crackers and... she looked to the table, there she saw herself when she was younger, and looked down at her feet, where Mary was, and back at the counter to see... to see...

Texas ran to the front door, threw it open, and ran to the street to see Fred at a steady jog making his way to her, screaming, "I figured it out! Texas, I'm sorry! But I figured it out."

Texas put her hair up with a piece of string on the counter and ran outside in her bare feet, still holding the plate.

"I'm sorry for the things I said." Fred began. He was dressed in shorts and flip-flops that seemed to slosh with each step. His hair was a bit unkept, but he had an intensity about him. "I know, I can't take it back-"

Texas hugged him tightly. "Fred, it's fine." Texas began. "I mean it, really. I have taken you for granted. I'm sorry." Texas brushed the red hair from her face, and they noted the silence. The bird stopped singing, the wind stopped blowing, and nothing crept into all the corners of the world. They straightened up and took a breath. They heard an engine rumble and several backfires and followed the sound.

Main Street was empty and, oddly, everyone was inside. The center of town held no banners, no fanfare, or closed-off streets, but rolling slowly through the road was a convertible humming a mechanical tune. Prometheus sat in the back with his hand gently waving at no one as Washington drove.

Fred and Texas ran up beside the car and laid their hands on the door. "Prometheus, you made it back?" Texas said. "I mean, obvious..." She added.

"Oh good, you're alive. Humans, my brothers and sisters, have made a right mess of everything. I am going home. I saw all the people waiting to take the town as soon as Asteria gives them the go-ahead. It is their world now, not mine." Prometheus waved to no one on the grass, specifically.

Fred looked at them, "What are you doing?"

"I'm waving." Prometheus said. Three eagles circled overhead and cawed, but this time Prometheus didn't duck or move.

"To whom?" Fred protested.

"To whoever. This is my giving-up wave. I don't know where to find the closet. Everyone who might have known was at the Grove. I am not in the fight anymore, and I'm saying goodbye to it all. It is time I go back to my rock." Prometheus turned his head and looked at the street corner. Texas and Fred made note of his glance but didn't see anything.

"So, who is over there?" Fred asked.

"No one yet. Sometimes you just have to do a thing because it's good to practice. There will be people who are happy to see me again, one day. We're heading to the wall and going to give up to the crowd."

"What crowd?" Fred asked.

"The crowd that is here for your key." Washington plainly said.

"What!? And what will they want with her key?" Fred was indignant.

"I don't know, but if they find you, they'll probably kill you." Prometheus said.

Texas was jogging beside the car, "We need to find the closet. You said you could find it, but–"

"I don't know where to begin. Everyone is dead..." Prometheus began. Washington looked over. "The world is burning, girl. We are trying to do something."

"But nothing." Said Texas, "We need to open the closet! That will stop everything. I will bring it all back."

"And what if you don't?" Washing barked. "Do you think you are the first key holder to go looking for the closet?"

Texas stood straight. She hadn't thought about it a lot.

"You're not unique!" Washing parked and got out of the car. "I had a key; I didn't go looking for the closet because I knew it could be used for so much more. I chose to start a machine, this, this, this nation, a system of government that was the great experiment. And you are going to use the key for what? The closet that you don't even know exists. How selfish."

Prometheus looked on. "It is a noble pursuit. But he is right. I have changed my mind."

"Of course I am right! What I built is being destroyed. We, those who also believe, have spent every last ounce we have on fitting a new broken machine, but we need a key; we need someone to start up, someone to run it. Abandon this."

Prometheus looked at her. Texas let a tear run down her face. Fred stepped in. "This isn't about you," He said, poking his finger at Washington.

"You're right. It isn't about me. It isn't about her, or you, it is about us! Us! All of us.

That was the whole point. But you go run off and find the closet." Washing ended. "I'm not being selfish," Texas said. "I'm not being selfish!" She said again.

"You are. Go out in the world this minute. It is falling apart, and use your key to fix the situation." Washing said and walked away.

"I'm going to open the closet!" Texas said. "And what? You have the power to fix this!"

Prometheus looked on, “Washington, please wait.” He looked at Texas and Fred. “Do either of you know how to drive?”

No one answered. “Right,” Prometheus said, “I guess I’m walking.” He hopped out of the car, and started walking off as the vehicle slowly drifted down the road and stopped when it bumped into a tree. “Follow me.” He said. Texas and Fred fell in step. “He is right, you know. I’m sure one of my brothers or sisters will make it easy for you.”

Prometheus took a breath and looked at Texas. “My rock…” He trailed off. “Where could it be? Where could the closet be?” he said thoughtfully. “Lumbini, Bodh Gaya, Franklin River, Varanasi…” he thought out loud. Fred and Texas looked at each other. “My rock taught me persistence. If I list all the cities, I will remember.” He said, shaking his head.

“What about Jerusalem?” Fred asked.

“There are a lot of Jerusalems.” They all stopped. They were at the edge of town somehow, and the crowd had grown larger and fiercer. The Lawyer had set up a tent with a small desk, and the woman with the dictionary was standing next to her, sorting papers as she thumbed through a large book.

“Asteria stopped by and gave me some money. We can travel anywhere.” Texas said.

Washington dared to put his toe on the chalk line and the crowd took a step forward. He took a step back. “Travel is closed.” Prometheus continued, “Zawiyet el Aryan would be best, but the Black Hills are closest.” He paused. “There is another place, but we will need permission.”

“Where is that?” Fred. “Shin-au-av”

They looked out at the crowd waiting to enter the town.

Later.

Prometheus looked up at the ceiling of the underground Masonic train that they were once again using to get from North Dakota to the eastern edge of Wyoming. Its musty smell of glory days still lingered, but this time, Prometheus had brought snacks.

“What are we doing again?” Fred asked.

“We are going to the Grand Tetons to see the nine unselfish. There we will gain entry to the Shin-au-av." Prometheus was lying on his back, the red velvet couch was matted on the arms, and the left cushion had a serious indent that made his head dip back. Texas was pacing, rolling his hair between his fingers, lunging every once in a while, and jumping to keep the nerves from getting to her.

"Where are the Grand Tetons?" This world is so weird, she thought. "They aren't far now," Prometheus said, closing his eyes.

The train was nearing a tunnel with a bump and returned to the track, flooding the cabin with light. Before them lay a long range of mountains that seemed to hold up the sky as they pierced the clouds. Their snow cap tips stood sentry over a lush, dense deciduous forest as long plains of grass stretched out carpeting the land. Overhead, a Western Meadowlark was having feelings about the cold winter ahead, but decided it was best to think of the bug that just flew past.

"This is amazing." Said Fred, "Where are we again?

"I told you, we're in Wyoming." Prometheus was gritting his teeth now. He bounced his fingers against one another, thinking of the road ahead.

Fred and Texas watched out the window. He moved his foot closer to hers, but she didn't move; she made it a point to keep her eyes on the horizon. "One day," Fred began, "It would be nice to live out here."

"No, I don't want that," Texas said.

"Oh, stop it. Why not?" Fred challenged her.

"Because I don't care, Fred, this whole thing has taught me I don't want to go out into the world, it's messy and absurd. I want to just go back home." She instinctively leaned close.

"How much did Asteria give you?" Fred felt the hair on his arms go up.

"Too much" Texas avoided the question.

"That sounds good. Think about it, Texas. No more worries." Fred dreamed.

"I don't have any worries before either."

The train pulled into the large mountain hole that went deep in the center. Large arches covered the structure as they saw the smooth side walls with pictures of people across the world that, at 192km/hr, told the story of comets, asteroids, triumphs, and then it slowed down to a single frame of a world covered in jungle.

A group dressed in simple white robes and smiles, greeting them from a grand platform that donned floating globes and twinkling lights. “Hello, I’m glad you could make it here. They have been expecting you.” They spoke like one and motioned with their hands as others brought over fresh fruit and grains. Prometheus responded with some complex hand gestures while holding himself straight with his head turned up and to the left. They mirrored his image. “Yes, of course.” The humans waved them on.

Texas, Fred, Washington, and Prometheus walked through the large cavern and into a long stone hall that extended a half mile straight to a staircase worn by millennia of steps.

Upon the top of the stairs, past many offshoots and closed doors, to a large platform at the center of the mountain, where there stood two large doors of plain stone with no gear or hinge.

As the stone moved, it revealed a room that was hollowed out so that most of the mountain was empty to the top, bridged by buttresses and supports made of living rock. There, nine large glowing beings stood around an open pit that emitted heat and brought the room up to body temperature.

There was a group of birdlike humanoids off to the side, their feathers so small that they looked like scales. They moved like a flock, distorted from the sheen of their skin, naked in their form and looking similar to reptiles. “Left over from the dinosaurs.” Washington said. “They don’t deal with people from the surface often.” Texas and the group stood before the glowing beings.

“We need to find Eden.” Prometheus boomed. His voice echoed off the cavernous chamber. “They are hard of hearing.” Prometheus whispered.

“What~” One said.

“I said, we need to find Eden.” Prometheus repeatedly gave his group an ‘ok’ sign.

“You didn’t let us finish.” There was a long pause “What for?” said no of the glowing beings said.

“We have a key holder.” Prometheus said. “I said, we have a Key Holder.” Texas waved her hand, greeting them.

Again, there was a pause. “There have been many key holders; none have gone to Eden.”

"I'm going to reset everything." Texas yelled. Her voice was barely a whisper. "Hello?" She yelled, but the cavern ate her words. "I'm going to let out God." There was a long pause.

"Then, no." One being said.

"But I need to." She pleaded

"You need to? God is not a genie." They said. "Go. We will not help."

There was a loud rumble, and the earth shook. Everyone paused. This time, the beings of light spun. "Seek the serpent in two days." They said.

The mountain quaked, and an eruption of sound echoed through the stone face, then a voice boomed. "Surrender yourself." It said. The beings of light blinked out as if someone flicked a switch. Everyone scattered. There was another quake as the mountain shook.

Prometheus yelled, "Follow me!" and ran for a large metal door that the robed people had opened. Down and through the corridors, following throngs of people out, they made their way to sunlight as the walls reverberated and echoed, shaking with each concussive boom.

Thanks to the natural gravitational pulls, the sun is six feet closer to the Earth in Jackson Hole and Nevada. Washington ran out and screamed, "My eyes!" before stopping Texas as Fred slammed into them. The missiles stretched across the sky as fingers scraping the stone monolith that is Table Mountain. Screams were heard, Texas stood up, and grabbed hold of Prometheus. "What is going on!?" She yelled.

They were on an outcropping of stone, halfway up the mountain, that was a natural ledge devoid of trees. Below them was the plains, dotted with trees and kicking up dust from the mountain's base. They could see the tracks their train came in on being pockmarked with explosions. There was a hum in the air, buzzing from an unseen bee, rocks and a dust filled cloud blanketed the ground, obscuring the crowd that had fanned out. Then it stopped.

"It is my brother," Prometheus said. They looked down on the plains to see a large cast of brown and green machines, dotted with soldiers at the ready. Air support heralded a cacophony that streaked the sky, strafing the ground, corralling the large groups of vehicles exiting from the mountain base. Texas and Fred watched from the ledge of the outcropping and heard a bugle call.

Washington stepped behind them. From the smoke came the Betsy Ross Flag, followed close behind by a group of monster trucks and citizens on horses. "Those rag-tag, stars and stripes!" George said. "The last great hope for the great experiment! Look there's Ben, and Thomas!"

A large green and tan monster truck peeled off and drove straight for the outcropping. George pulled out a mirror and flashed it up and down, reflecting the sun. Below, the missiles started firing, and the two bodies engaged in smoke and earth.

George waved everyone on. "Come" He shouted. Prometheus starts followed by Fred and Texas. Washington would stop sporadically flashing his mirror and running down a loose path with everyone until a large truck met them. Out popped Martha, in a blue gown, and grabbed George, kissing him hard on the lips. She handed him a musket, "Let's go!" Martha and George looked at Prometheus, "Take the truck." She said. "We'll run down."

Prometheus got in the truck, "Texas, Fred, get in! We have to go, now." Texas and Fred jumped into the cab. "George–" Texas began.

"I told you," George started. "I used my key on this–"

"George!" Martha yelled as she ran down the hill, musket in hand, beckoning him on. He followed.

Prometheus revved the engine and drove South, Texas, and Fred watched as George and Martha made their way down the Mountain thirty feet before someone rode up with two horses in tow for them. They mounted and off to the front they went.

"Where are we going now?" Texas asked.

"South, to Shin-au-av," Texas and Fred looked at Prometheus. "You know it as Area 51." An Eagle overhead cawed.

CHAPTER 26

"The nonsense has a purpose. If you only paid attention,"

[Harold Van deCombe]

The mountain gave way as a range to dry, red Earth as they sped South, "Faster!" Prometheus said as they sped up. When they passed the Roswell diner, their truck was running on fumes and starting to sputter before coughing up black soot and rolling to a stop.

They jumped out. "Follow," Prometheus commanded as he started to run ahead.

They had been walking for 10 miles but not getting anywhere, as the land didn't seem to change. The sun was now 8 feet closer to the Earth, and Texas could feel her hair sizzle as each breath exhaled precious water. Prometheus seemed fine, unfazed by the travel, pacing several feet in front of them. Fred was furthest behind, keeping quiet, trying not to let on that he could feel his muscles contract and his calves seize up. There was a pop in his head, and he felt like soda being shaken up, letting the bubbles out as he made his way to the ground.

Texas turned "Fred!" She said as she too buckled from the heat and dropped.

There was no time. They woke up to the bump of a flat bed, and a kind old woman, sun-kissed with leathery skin, was squeezing water into their mouths via a clean cloth. The old woman whispered Askulai lolmani and squeezed another round of warm water in Texas's mouth. Texas turned over to see Fred stirring but unchanged. She felt her skin was on fire, her pale white features shriveling in the heat of the sun. The flatbed stopped, and Texas sat up looking all around to see–

The border of Shin-au-av was covered with people, the reptile bird people glowed in the radiant sunlight, their small, luminescent feathers were like beacons. She heard the car truck door open and Prometheus's voice say kwakwha and the old woman responded askwali. The eagles circled high above.

Prometheus hopped up and sat beside Texas, lifting her up a little and handing her a cup of water from the bowl the woman was using. "Here, drink up." He said. Texas leaned forward, and the old woman jumped down and joined a small group of people equally sun-drenched, walking toward an outcropping of rocks with a large metal hanger door embedded in the side.

Prometheus jumped down. "I'm going to see if I can see the stars."

"It's day…Who are these people?" Said Texas, lifting Fred, feeding him water.

"Not now. Like later. They are the Naga, a remnant from the dinosaurs."

"You can see the stars anytime! Why here?" Texas yelled.

"You don't get it!" Prometheus said, walking away.

Texas took a look around and noticed they were at a gatehouse with the reptile bird creature ushering people in. Texas helped Fred up. "Where…" Fred started. "It's okay." Texas soothed him, holding him up and walking him in with the group. From behind, four large buses of people barreled in and the small group that Texas was with moved to the side. The Naga guard kept pointing to move everyone forward. A young woman said, "Thank you, Anu Naki."

"I thought they were the Naga?" Fred whispered. "Let's just keep going. I lost Prometheus." Texas said.

"Hey, I wonder where Gabby and the Angels are?" Fred questioned. "Probably saving ice cream from the sun. Could you imagine them here?"

Prometheus was ahead, the road gave way to a large concrete slab, and as they walked closer to the hangar, they could see a contingent of Feathered reptiles coming out of the open hangar door. The one in the lead had a plume about his head, and every couple of steps, they looked up to see an eagle overhead.

Prometheus looked back at Texas and Fred and waved them forward. "Lord Quetzalcoatl, I need to see the night sky." Prometheus began. The Naga didn't say a word.

"I will obey the treaty, but it is the only way I can find Eden."

They looked at him, "The nine unselfish have retreated back, and so are we. You can have the surface and see where they get you." They kept looking at the sky as if they were waiting for something, to see something. But it was the sound that caught their attention first. An explosion occurred about four miles away in the mountain range. The explosion wasn't one of combustion but one of a balloon collapsing in on itself if it were the size of Manhattan. The reptiles all squawked.

"We are closing our access points." Quetzalcoatl said. "Do not follow us to

Agartha." Prometheus looked back and gave the thumbs up to Texas and Fred.

A missile flew overhead, missing the whole of the group, careening into a rock face off in the distance. Black helicopters were closing, and from the shimmering horizon a sea of mechanical vehicles appeared. "You brought destruction on us!" Quetzalcoatl said. A flood of Naga came from the hangar doors, scooping people and bringing them into the hangar.

Texas and Fred ran with the group but were pulled by the Naga out. "You're not allowed in." A Naga said.

"We need safety!" Fred said.

A concussive hit 200 meters away and blew them down causing a ringing in their ears. Texas saw the Naga pointing off in the distance to buses racing to the caves, one was smoking. They bent down as a flock and sprinted to the smoking caravan.

There were five Humvees sprinkling the buses' tires with bullets, trying to stop them, but Uranus dropped from the sky as a meteor, smashing the ground and throwing the vehicles in the air. The buses took advantage of the speed. The Reptiles stopped and whispered Masauwu for he was to devour the world. Everyone knew of Uranus.

The three buses were able to gain distance, as the Naga intercepted and jumped onto the sides of the bus, arching their backs and reflecting the sun. As if small lighthouses, they threw off the heat sensors and the Humvees that were still behind them.

Texas watched on as she saw a wall of light and fire push through the dessert, and like ants a line of the vehicle burst into flames.

CHAPTER 28

"You hide truth in lies"
[Most people]

The Earth moved and shook as if on a trampoline, bouncing people and equipment. The dissonance was so mixed and interspersed that panic took hold. It looked as if ants were scurrying after boiling water was poured directly on their hill. The Naga closed ranks as they ushered more people into the hangar doors.

The buses sped into the opening, the last of the groups, as shells littered the ground. Uranus was running at the entrance, as the ordinances were now firing upon him without any effect. Bouncing as a cartoon across the ground, letting each foot fall reverberate as a small quake upon the surface of Earth. A fault line 2 miles away started to shudder and could feel its grip loosening.

A mining shaft opened up underneath a tank and punched up Earth, displacing the large metal frame before cracking it down. There were squeals as the last of the Naga flittered for the pockmarked ground to the hub.

The entire army turned their weaponry upon Uranus as he started to go through the column of armored vehicles. The Apache helicopters flew up beside him and opened up as the guns played a song of death, their snare drum like bullets pepper the ground and bounced off him.

Then he reached down and put his hand in the Earth, and there was a shake as small holes started to open up and steam poured out. Hot water deep within the Earth boiled as magma shot up through pinpricks of the sand. Each one takes the Apache from below, tearing small poles as if with a shotgun.

The string of Mountains looked as if it was folding up. A papier-mache stone facade with steep angles became more like boxes folding in on themselves, over and over again, trying to flatten out with the rest of the landscape. Quetzalcoatl made a sweeping motion with his hand and disappeared into the puzzle that was descending into the Earth.

There was a crash, and it was as if thunder and lightning collided all at once, and the ground slipped and shifted as another army came into view. This time it was the priests, the

Swiss guard were occupied on a beach in Cabo and fundraising efforts. So, instead old men with their canes and their walkers, several on scooters, entered the fray and headed right for Texas. Fred grabbed her hand, her heart fluttered, and they started to run.

The mountain stopped, a large bus barreling in. Fred saw the hangar door open again.

Texas outpaced Fred running toward the entrance.

Rockets traveled across the sky, one pierced the side of the mountain that was opening, shaking fiercely, trying to stay above ground long enough for the bus. Fire shot up in a spurts, and the flames spread out, dancing with the torrents of dust. Then a young woman came running out, flanked by two Naga grasping at her as if to pull her back in. They grabbed hold of her flannel shirt and tore off the right sleeve. She broke away and stumbled. The woman brushed off the dust from her torn jeans and cut skin. Texas could see an outline under the woman's tee-shirt, it was cylindrical in nature with an unlocky bit...

Texas squeezed Fred's hand and turned her eyes to the woman, The Naga held out their hands as if begging the woman to stay but she kept running forward and from the back, a tall figure, like the one of the unselfish, but nine feet, bright as the sun, moving at the speed of thought, shimmered and popped in front of her. The area under her feet glistened like Texas had seen with the Asteria. The woman pulled the curtain of reality open, just slightly, to reveal what looked like the beginning of a large engine. A part of the machine jetted out and had a small lock in it.

The woman placed the key within the lock and turned it; the sun dimmed. Clouds appeared and darkened, and lightning descended from the sky. A torrent of storms descended upon the desert, tornadoes touched down, bottling up vehicles and large swaths of soldiers and priests. It was indiscriminate and took out people from all areas, picked up dust, and threw it in the eyes of all, so they could hardly see their fingers in front of their faces. The woman fell down, her eyes opened, unmoving. The Naga grabbed her and pulled her back.

Texas screamed, "I think she's dead!"

"Was she a key holder?" Fred exclaimed.

"Is that what the key does? Is that what the key does?" Texas was on repeat.

The wind howled and everything started to shake. Uranus's hand grabbed Texas and lifted her high into the air before she knew he was even near her. Fred instinctively went low and then threw his shoulder into Uranus's waist. It was stone. Uranus wouldn't budge; Fred would have a better chance of moving a mountain. "I will give you the chance to destroy everything with me," Uranus said. "I will give you the chance to remake all, for that is my role. I'm the one who unmakes so that we can remake it. Imagine all that we could do." He shouted, as the wind yelled, throwing anything without roots in the air.

Fred jumped up on Uranus's arm, trying to pull him down. The ground shook again as the last of the mountains became flat and the Naga retreated beneath the Earth. The atmosphere ionized, wafting the smoke of ozone to the four corners. "It's not worth saving anyway," Uranus began, staring directly at Fred. "You're not sad, none of this is worth fighting for, none of this is worth dying for, and opening the closet will only make it worse." And with that, he reached down and flicked Fred off of him. Fred went limp as his body hit the ground, and his shoulder folded in on itself as his head snapped back. His body rolled before being clipped by two sharp stones, and the ground opened up in front of him and swallowed him.

A woman with a clipboard showed up next to Uranus. He pointed to the mouth chasm and briskly said, "He's over there." Texas screamed, lifted her legs, and kicked him in the face, chest, arms, and anywhere about the body where her feet could reach, but it did nothing.

Uranus didn't move. "This is what happens when you try to control things." He said, "You're better off not participating." Texas took the key from her neck and held it over her head to throw, but saw–

On Uranus's bicep, there was a keyhole. She paused, "And I will turn this world into a desolate paradise upon which all things will disappear." He began with a villain's monologue. Texas felt her vision blur as the pounding of her heart hit her head, and the lightning cracked all around her. She took the handle of the key, looked at Fred, or where he should have been. She cried, shaking in tears, alone once again; she realized what she had lost before she even knew what she had, and she took the key and plunged it towards his arm before Uranus's hand covered the keyhole. Texas looked up to see a bright flash as lightning struck her, and she flew from his hand as a dove who defied the wind, landing gently on the ground. She took a dust-filled breath and exhaled into the darkness.

Chapter 29

"Plants follow the same pattern. All life follows the same pattern"

[School Book, 1892]

Texas rubbed her eyes, and from darkness came light, first a sharp brilliance that drowned out the world, and slowly the darker bits and the larger bits became whole and morphed and coalesced into the scene before her. There was a voice quietly saying You're OK, you're OK. Texas turned her head to the sound of the voice to see a figure wreathed in light, smelling of holly, pine, and flowers. And there was a heavy rose scent that inappropriately rubbed upon her.

Her eyes watered, and every bit of her hurt. Her brain was fuzzy, static, not connected, no Wi-Fi; it was as if each thought was floating away, not coming into focus until Fred, his face, flashed in front. It moved away as a cloud dispersed by a gust of wind, "Fred!" Texas screamed.

Gia once again said You're OK, you're OK, which caused Texas's hands to squeeze and push upon the ground, thrusting her up to a sitting position. You're OK her lips didn't move.

"I know I'm OK," Texas said. "I'm asking about Fred." The lighted figure came into focus.

A woman, human, but her skin was almost metallic in nature; it would reflect pieces of the sun in blues, greens, oranges, and yellows, so slight that you would never know if you were standing far away or close. Like watching a living tapestry of the Earth, Texas watched on in splendor.

"Are you an Angel?" Texas asked.

"No." She said, "those are terrible. They never know what they're doing, and they always have questions like children."

Texas was still in the desert, her chest clenched, and her heart picked up pace. She looked down to see cuts, bruises, and her left foot at an unnatural angle. Sweat started to bead upon her forehead, and the image and feeling of a hand around her throat, hatred gripping~ Gia put her hand upon Texas's shoulder, and Texas was immediately relieved. She could feel the radiance as if someone on a warm day were pressing against her skin and pushing out from her through each nerve and fiber. She found her veins open, and each capillary was filled with what felt like excitement. Each bone aligned, while each muscle relaxed, the skin sewed itself shut, and she felt a weighted blanket upon her shoulders, as her eyes closed, "Don't fall asleep." Texas opened her eyes and looked again at the woman.

Looking past Gia was Uranus laying on the ground, the man who had chased them for days now, his dark hair was matted and strung upon the ground, snoring heavily, his body quietly twitching in the sun as if it were the softest bed.

Luna came up beside her, but instead of holding gas, she held water, a large gallon jug of it. She leaned down gently and took Texas's hand, pouring water, washing, then cupping them and pouring a small mouthful of water. "Drink up," she said. Texas looked up. The land was barren and flat again. The Naga were gone, the war was gone, the army was gone, all was gone except for her, some women, and a snoring Uranus.

"Where is everybody?" Texas asked. "Where's Fred!?" The woman looked at Texas, and she shook her head. Luna looked at her and leaned in to give her a hug. "Where is everybody?" Texas asked.

Gia said, "Gone. We moved them on, or we returned them from whence they came. All is back the way it was before. The women were walking around, taking long walking sticks and burying the shafts into the ground, bringing up spring water while planting flowers, making the barren earth dotted with green.

"What are you doing?" Texas asked, and Gia simply said, "We have a lot of healing to do. Hopefully, we can get in front of it."

Fred. Not now. "Who is he?" Texas asked, staring at Uranus.

"He likes to destroy; I like to create; it's a good relationship." Gia said. "I'm glad I stopped you before you used your key on him."

Texas clasped her neck and followed her finger to the key still attached to the cord. She wobbled, wavered, and then stood up. "There was a key holder, another one, and she died!" Texas said.

"Everyone dies." Gia said.

"Well, I don't want to die." Texas stated.

"No one ever really does," Gai began, "but you were given a key and use it or don't, the end is the same, the only difference is whatever you were supposed to unlock ~ we'll have to wait for someone other than you."

"What does this unlock?" Texas asked.

Gia shrugged, "I don't know, it's never been my specialty." The woman shook her head, glimmering in the light. "Come," And Gia took Texas's hands, and once again she felt the energy shoot through her body as her feet moved easily, gliding almost as they walked to what was at one time a barren desert, was now an orchard of trees. One of which that sprang forth was an avocado tree bearing ripe fruit, she handed it to Texas. "Am I supposed to eat this?"

"Yes, don't you like fruit?"

Texas poked at it. "Yes, but I would like an apple or an orange."

"I think you need an avocado."

"I don't really know how to eat an avocado, unless it's on toast, or in salsa, or on a chip." Texas said.

"You know, you humans are never happy." She paused and said, "Yes, but that wouldn't help people." And continued, "Didn't you see I just created all of this out of nothing? We have brought forth water springs from the ground where it was once deserted. Green and lush, and now you're complaining that it's not the lush you want."

"I didn't mean to offend, and I didn't mean to–" Texas tried to defend herself.

"I know you didn't, but you did." Gia said.

In another time and place.

Fred was a child again, running around his parents' coffee house as he had eaten a handful of espresso beans and felt like he could both fly and throw up all at once, which is what he did. He put his arms up and ran around, occasionally stopping at the corner, until his mother and father saw him and picked him up.

Then he was really flying, talking, sharing, and doing anything that he could do as his body shook with caffeine. Fred A voice said. Quietly, he knew the voice. He knew the sound. He could smell something. It was sulfur-like. Eggs, someone was cooking. He wasn't in the coffee house anymore; he was camping with his father. The crack of the fire in the forest, and he heard a rustle in the woods and the shuffle of the leaves, and he felt loved.

He heard the voice again, but he couldn't find out where it was coming from. Fred. The voice became closer, and he felt a hand clasping his shoulder as he turned around to see Mary. Lovely Mary. But, she was young and old all at once. It was as if she was transitioning between ages; sometimes unknown, sometimes like he saw her yesterday, but never the same.

"You have to stay in the moment, focus. Give me your thoughts." She said.

Fred and she were once again in another area of his life, this time, he must have been a baby, but he was conscious. He couldn't see where he was; it was just an apartment. He was staring at the ceiling, and Mary was leaning over him. "Fred, you have to stay in one place. Think of my house." The front of Mary's house came into view.

"We're on the porch." Mary said, and they were on the porch, only this time he was sitting. Now he was sitting on the floor cross-legged, and then he was sitting on a chair, and then he was pacing, and Mary said, "You need to think of a single moment. A single thought."

And he was there, singularly, and Mary sat beside him in an old rocking chair. She had her hand in his, "It's so lovely to see you! Did you go to college? Did you have kids? I have so many questions. You must have had such a full life." She was straining to keep her thoughts focused. "Did you see Texas? Sorry," she said, "what's the last thing you remember?"

And they were in the desert amongst the fires, amongst the cacophony of human bodies being pulled apart, and there was Fred being flung forth. Texas is being choked and her screams and... clap. They were back at Mary's house on the porch and sat in silence.

"Where am I?" Fred asked.

Mary grabbed him, "Show me Texas!" She pleaded. "Is Texas here? I need to see..." And they went back to the place, but this time it was no longer the desert, but instead the place where Gia had plucked the avocado. "I think you need an avocado." The woman said. Mary's heart was ruined and melted simultaneously, and Gia turned her head, staring directly at Mary.

"What are you doing here?" Fred said, "Where is the dessert? Avocados." Fred mused.

"You know, you humans are never happy." Gia said.

"You could charge a lot of money for these," Fred said staring at the avocados.

"Yes, but that wouldn't help people." Gai said and touched Fed's head, and Fred and Mary were back on her porch and joined by another tall, strong man dressed in linen, smiling, holding a tray of lemonade, which he handed out dutifully. "Where were you?" he said

They both looked at him, and Mary started, "Hello, I'm Mary. What's your name?" Atlas Shrugged, "I go by several. I'm a friend of Texas, have you seen her?" Mary and Fred looked at each other.

Fred knew him. He was from somewhere, maybe a...

"Yes." Mary said, "We were just in the desert, but it's not a desert now, there are trees, I don't know, things are so strange here. If you can't keep your thoughts together, you tend to wander, and it makes it hard to see."

"Yes, it's very strange." Atlas sat down before them, pulling up a chair that wasn't there a moment before and looking them in the eyes. He held his hands and said, "I can give you everything, you understand? I can give you anything and everything if you would only just tell me where Texas is."

500 million popped in Fred's head. Five hundred–He knew. This was the villain speaking. For who else would give things in exchange for people rather than save people in exchange for things?

"I could give you gold," and from Atlas's hand he produced gold out of thin air, then coins and diamonds, rubies and sapphires, and any number of things, and Fred stood in silence.

Mary was frozen but smiled as if she had been stunned and caught in place by some invisible force. Fred, being clever, looked at the gold and said, I want to stop him in his head. "I want a powerful weapon, I want something more powerful than you could ever dream of, and I want it to be more powerful than you." Fred began.

Atlas held his hands and took him to a place in the desert. There was a mountainous region, warm and dry, and several rocks came down the side of the rock face, clicking and clasping after one another, and a spark from the rocks ignited a nearby bush. Atlas walked over and bent down, the flames whispered something nondescript and descript all at once, and yet so loud that Fred could barely catch his breath, for the sound was as if the air had been sucked from his lungs and water poured in his ears. When he opened his eyes, Atlas had brought out what looked like a horn, curled in nature, and made of bone. "All right," He handed it to Fred, "Here, blow on this ram's horn and heroes of ages past will come. Heroes that cannot be defeated. They will be so strong that they will fight any and every battle for you."

Fred thought. He took the horn and told him, "I don't know where Texas is." Clever, Fred thought.

Atlas gently touched Fred's head, and a white thread appeared that extended far into the distance. Atlas touched it, and when he did, Fred saw Texas in all his memories, but this time, Atlas was in the back, looking, intruding. Fred was willing the memories back to just him and her but Atlas plucked it like a guitar string. "Where your mind is focused, there go your thoughts." Atlas closed his eyes and gave two more taps. "There you are."

Chapter 29, Part 2

"Knowing yourself is the beginning of all wisdom"

[Aristotle]

If you were a satellite high above the ground, soaring as a Fumble (you're species will learn of them in 139 years when one is discovered around the moon, Callisto), you would see dots of flames licking the sky where cities once were. You would also see large groups of people moving in herds of caravans. People bartering goods and toilet paper, which is now a surprising luxury.

You would also find a place that was domed and covered in marble, glittering, and you would see a man named Kronos diligently at his desk, writing, and writing, creating edicts and laws that had no real bearing on anything. That was all pulled from the ether itself, but people would look at them and think to themselves This is good. I will follow this. While others would say, This is terrible and I will not follow it. To which other people would say, I'd follow this made-up rule, though it's unjust. And others would say, I don't care, I just want pizza back.

He would continue to write these laws, and these laws would contradict one another, and that contradiction would cause more consternation, and more big words. So, the people would start fighting with one another over what laws were true and what laws were right, or just, or good, or bad, not realizing they were all just made up. Kronos sat in his high tower, which nearly reached to the heavens, but was unfinished, and he penned paper and–

Atlas came in and sat across from him. They both looked at one another, "Have you found her yet?"

"I might have a lead," Atlas said, pulling himself up and walking to a corner of the room, bent down, and flicked his finger at the air, as if peeling up a sticker from nothing. He grasped the corner of reality and pulled gently, trying not to tear anything. He opened up a small area and peeked behind the curtain of reality; it waffled. Behind large machines, churning and biting bits of metal spun; he could hear them rusting and grinding against one another. As if someone had forgotten to oil the gears. There wasn't a bottle of grease big enough.

Kronos was still at his desk writing without thoughts or concern. Kronos started, "We need the key, the machines need the key." Atlas smiled and said, "Yes, I understand what it takes to run the world, for it has been upon my shoulders forever."

Texas sat around the fire with a group of other women, each dressed in white. Luna brought over a large bowl of salad and individual plates full of beans. Gia sat beside her as they were in a forest that seemed to weave a house out of branches and leaves. Animals sat beside them: the bear, the snake, and the eagle, but each was respectful of the others and would not eat one another in front of her.

"I need to find Eden." Texas said.

"You need to get to Eden?" Gia laughed, "Why would you ever need to go there. Can't you see where we are? This is paradise."

"I need to get to Edan in order to let God out of the closet."

"You don't want to do that," Gia said.

"Well, why not?" Asked Texas.

Gia smiled and said, "The closet has been locked for so long, do you think that whatever comes out of it would actually know what to do? That which has been locked away is no longer a part of the world. It's up to us to make this, and I am making a wonderful paradise. I am creating something the likes of which no one will ever understand, but all will love.

Texas thought about Gia's words. "So, you know the closet, and what it's about?"

"I do. I know heaven and Earth, and I know the depth of hell as well, Texas." Gia leaned in. "I'm creating a world for I am the steward, no one else."

"I don't think I fully understand what it is you're going to get out of this?" Texas asked.

"Who said I have to get anything... Why does anyone have to get something? We should just be." Gia said. "And, you shouldn't open the closet."

"If I can open up the closet and I could be with my mom again; it can be quiet, and peaceful, and I can sleep like I would–"

Gia interjected, "That will never happen." Each word touched upon the feeling of calm, turning it into caution and concern; the hint laid a threat as if there were knives upon each syllable, and the sharpness of the words pierced each part of her skin. She knew they were true, and she knew that Gia was correct, that from her nothing would be fixed, that opening the closet would give her nothing. She shrugged that off.

"No, that's not true; it is not true. When I open up the closet, everything will be right, and I can make a wish upon the stars, and God will be thankful, and I can ask whatever I want, and it will arrive in the snap of its fingers." Texas squeezed her hands. "I will open the closet and create heaven on earth."

"I don't think people really understand heaven." Gia began. "What does it look like?" Texas hadn't stopped to look around. Everyone was talking, laughing. They all had enough to eat. The forest provided food, shelter, and the animals lived in harmony. "If this were a story, do you think people would want to read this?"

Texas looked at her and shook her head. "I'm looking for more than heaven. I'm looking for that thing I had when I was a kid. When I could do what I want."

"So, you're not looking for peace. You're looking for no responsibility. Which is probably one of the reasons you don't want to use your key. The key brings a lot of responsibility to it. It can do more than just open up the closet. It could do a great many things if you only knew." Gia said.

Gia turned and moved her face close to Texas's, kneeling beside her. A spring sprang in the Earth to her left, and Gia gently took one of Texas's feet, "Your feet are so dirty," and she pulled up water from the spring, gathered it in a moss sponge, and started washing her feet.

"I had a friend once; she was a lovely woman. And she had a key. And at the time, no one would allow keys to come from people like her, you know the intelligent ones. And she found heaven, not God, but in fact, she made heaven. She didn't even need to open up the closet. She was able to create it based on everything she had, and everything she knew, and you know what she did when she was there? She invited everybody to be with her. They all were happy... happy for a moment, and then the next moment, you know what they did? They got bored. And when they got bored, you know what they did? They destroyed that heaven.

"See, that's what boredom is, that's what heaven is, they're one and the same. When you are bored, you have everything you need in life. It means that you are not worried. You have all you need. And what happens then?" Gia leaned in. "Don't answer." Everyone became quiet.

The animals were standing now, and the women were quietly leaving the fires. "You become bored. And what happens when you're bored? You start messing around, and you start seeing what you can do, and you start fixing things that were never broken. Destroying and creating and everything else in between. You don't want to open up a closet, you don't want to create heaven on Earth, and you don't want to go back to a moment in time where you had no responsibility."

"I don't want–" Texas stood up.

"And do what? How long will that last? You don't understand the world, Texas. You don't understand." Gia rose up, and she was a light in the shadow. The animals around the fire no longer promise to keep calm as they bared their teeth and took their eyes from the fire. Snarling, they bit one another, clawing and attacking, taking chunks of flesh as the vines started choking out the life of the plants. The bugs came swarming as the mushrooms ate the decay, and from Gia came death and change. Forever change, forever strength, ever moving like water. A torrent like some sort of flood that would come through and wipe everything away, and recreate and rebuild, only to be destroyed again. Her body twisted, and ripping from beneath came something like Uranus. Luna grabbed Texas. "We need to leave now."

Texas screamed, but Luna covered her mouth. "When I said you need to leave, you need to leave. I will take care of her." Gia was reasserting herself, but a storm of biblical proportions descended upon them, and the sky darkened.

Gia felt the human touch again. Luna hugged her, and the creative energy slowed and quieted her down, but that did not stop the animals; they saw Texas, and they thought lunch. Texas knew she could no longer be here and ran, and ran, and ran, and as far as she could; she did not know where to go through a forest of cascading trees and branches that sounded familiar and unfamiliar with birds rustling flittering from branch to branch and creatures scattering under her feet. Then the sun shone through the branches, and a clearing emerged. Texas heard the gnashing and baying behind her and ran to a thicket, but stumbled on a patch of earth.

She rolled under the thorny fingers of the bush and into a cave that was hidden behind the shrub. She crawled forward. There was a whimper from what sounded like a wolf stuck with a thorn. She heard drips of water but kept crawling forward in fear, away from the intense rustling. Her eye adjusted to the grey formless cavern she found herself in, holding the ground, she gingerly found a wall and slowly walked along the hard surface.

There was a pinprick of light ahead, and slowly, bit by bit, one by one, the next thing she knew, the pinprick was a dime, then a quarter, and finally an opening. It was a cathedral in stone that grew in size as she moved toward the entrance. It was larger than any building she'd ever seen, and when she got to the sunlight and the mouth of the mammoth cave, she saw before her a series of mounds. More like pyramids made of earth, one of which was a giant snake. Its head and eyes pointed toward the east, and its body, writhing and slithering, pointed South.

Upon this grassy Knoll shaped as the Serpentine, was Prometheus.

Later.

Bob and Felicity, bloodied and tattered had been running for what felt like days until they collapsed upon a river's edge. Felicity buried her face in the water to wake up and then rolled over upon the stony shore and lay down to rest. Bob collapsed on all fours and took sips from the clean, clear water, taking deep breaths. His mission had failed, he was not able to stop Texas, he was not able to change anything, and over the last two or three attempts that he has tried, he has lost everything.

He set out on the darkest path of the forest from the castle in Dunmore, Rule 1, and it now led to the darkest part of his life. He said to himself, "What do I do now?" He looked down at the water to see his reflection and then asked again, "What do I do now?" From the back of his throat, from somewhere deep, he tasted pennies, and a metallic acid crept up his throat. It was a quiet vomit, something where he could feel the metal on slide across his tongue, and then quietly drop into the water. It lay upon stone; Bob reached down and grabbed it.

It felt as if the world were closing in on him, and things started to move slowly until he heard the sound of children, choral tones, the likes of which he knew.

The Angel came down beside him and said, "Did you ask a question?" and Bob made a heavy sigh. "I hate angels," he said to himself.

Later.

Prometheus and Texas sat on the head of the serpent and looked at the sky. "I'm sure she said Eden. So, you don't know where that is?" Prometheus shook his head no. "Sort of. This place will help with that. But I'm at the wrong time. I need to be here when the sun rises around the equinox in order to see which way the serpent's eyes would look, but it's just a Tuesday, and nothing special ever happens on a Tuesday."

"So, what do we do now?" Texas asked.

"I have one other idea, but it's a long shot. We have to go back to North Dakota." And Texas shuttered.

"To Nowhere?" she asked.

"The Black Hills." He responded.

Chapter 29, Part 3

"The only journey is the one within"

[Rainer Maria Rilke]

As hunters would do, if they had large prey hiding in the brush, they set fire to the grass.

But these fires wouldn't be indiscriminate; they wouldn't try to take out everything and anything. In fact, it would be a controlled burn; they would dig a trench around an area, and then they would set fire to the perimeter of it so that it would slowly engulf the space that they had outlined. And thereby draw out the prey into the line of sight.

That was Atlas's thought, but instead of a brush, he would use the rest of the United States, and he would start at one end, burning and slashing, and then at the bottom, and go back to the sides to push his prey to the center, where he needed them to be. But instead of using fire, he would use things like guns, bombs, and, well, I guess fire... I was wrong, he was using fire after all... and all manner of terrible things.

He would set his most insidious plan into action, for who needs to set fire when you can set a mind ablaze, so all he would do is point the finger. He would say to the people: "You are not to blame; you have done nothing wrong." To every single one. He would say, in fact, your anger is justified, your anger is important, and you are a great person, no matter how you act, no matter what you say, no matter what you do, no matter what you think, no matter how horrible an idea you might have; it was perfect.

In fact, if everybody thought like you, the world would be in a better place, but it's not in a good place, and it's not because of you or your actions, but because of other people. Specifically, this one person named Texas. Texas wasn't enough for some. So, he fanned that flame and made them feel so important, so smart, so intelligent, though those people had no idea about the world in which they lived.

Atlas made them feel good about that, and he would go on talk shows, and he would go on TV, and he would make people feel good about being angry, and he would tell them to point the finger. That's what he did, he pointed the finger left, right, and center, then eventually, once everybody was angry enough, he could point the finger at Texas. He knew this, the Titans knew this, and so it began.

The newscaster began, "Buffalo has fallen. It's the eighth city to burn due to being run by a bunch of stupid simpletons. We now go to the White House spokesperson."

She was pretty, with brown hair, put together, nails done, makeup on, she smiled a vibrant smile, and said quietly to everyone, "While we are all suffering, you have to understand that the rest of the world has not provided any aid. We are now at war with Canada and Mexico, as both see the US as weak. They were to take our border towns, like Buffalo. They are directly under attack by sympathizers. This is all being orchestrated by a single person–" and the picture of Texas flashed upon the screen. "Her name is Texas Rhodes. She comes from a long line of dissidents who want to see America fall, but we will not let that happen. What I'm charging each and every loyal citizen to do is go out and find this woman; she is the nation's top priority, and take her alive." And, with that, usually before hearing the word alive, most people would turn off their TVs, gather up all the weaponry in their house, and start the search.

Along the Pacific Coast, in the northernmost area, Gabby and Raph were flying high in the sky, looking for Jesus. "Why would he be this far north? Jesus always liked the sun and the sea. I think he would be in the South, maybe Southern California. It is such a gorgeous place. I was there the other week, and I tell you, there were no clouds in the sky. In fact, it was so blue I got kind of weird because there were zero clouds in the sky. Did you know that there were zero clouds in the sky, Raph?"

Ralphael, who was sort of listening, said, "Yes, I heard you. I know it rains a lot, but I really think Jesus is here because Jesus is all about the forest. He loves nature, and he loves trees," but they were interrupted as wings flew between the two of them, it was Michael yelling, "Fools! Have you not read any of the apocrypha, any of the books? Jesus grew up in the area that was desolate and dark, and I know exactly where he is. Follow me!"

They glided from the trees to the beach, to the ocean waves, and there, under the water, came a squid, eyes saucer-sized, three feet in diameter. It was an enormous, hulking mass of a squid. They stopped, "Look, here's Jesus!" Michael said, pointing at the squid. It looked up at them. The angels were tiny Suns to its view.

"That's not Jesus," Gabby said.

"Yes, it is, look, it is the same shape as the Pope's hats." Ralph reminded everyone.

"Did you know that the hats the Popes wear are called miter hats, and that's because they were in the shape of a fish. Fish is the symbol of the church because it's the symbol of Jesus. You feed people with fish." Michael's knowledge dumped.

Uriel swooped in, "Fish people came from the sea and taught humans agriculture."

The squid looked up at them. "It is definitely Jesus. The best Jesuses don't actually say anything. Gabby said. There was a pause and Gabby continued, "So, if the best Jesus says nothing, then maybe we don't need Jesus." They all looked at one another and shook their heads in agreement and flew off.

Texas and Prometheus were in the northernmost parts of North Dakota along the trail edges of the Black Hills. One of several places that the world began. Prometheus had a sextant and was looking at the night sky while Texas was on her back, trying to quiet from the panic that she almost always felt gripping her. A convocation of eagles waited on the branches, watching for the moment Prometheus's liver would be available.

At this point in time, she kept focused on the idea that if she could open up the closet, if she could just get to Eden, bring back her mother and Fred, then she could bring back everything, and she could close off the walls of Nowhere, and she could make it peaceful again. She realized that, for once and all, this world was scary; she should have listened to her mom and never left.

Prometheus looked up at the northern sky, made calculations, and looked upon Venus and Mars. "Texas, did you know that the earth wobbles and then it points to different constellations and that is how we move through the great year?"

"No. Will this help us find Eden?" Texas said rubbing her temples.

"I forgot that's what we were looking for, so now my calculations are completely off." And he went back to his paper, and he scribbled everything down, starting over again.

Texas saw the first star to the left of Venus and made a wish: help.

There was a rustle in the hills. They turned to see two hikers walking by. The two made it to the top of the hill, and illuminated by the morning rays, they saw Texas and Prometheus sitting upon the rocks with their sextant and azimuth, and trying to figure out which star was directly aligned and when Venus crested. The first wave followed by the second.

But those hikers have been watching the news, and they knew Texas, and they saw their opportunity for the government bounty. So, they took out their knives and whatever they could find, screamed, because that is what you do when you charge, and ran straight at them.

Prometheus shrugged and sat calmly as Texas recoiled back, crab walking and scrambling to get up. "We have to run." Texas said.

"Can't. We'll miss our chance." Prometheus said as he stayed seated.

One of the hikers unshouldered a rifle, and the other kept running. The barrel pointed in the general direction of Texas and fired. Texas did not see a hit. The hunter slung the rifle around their shoulder again and resumed the chase.

"Prometheus!" Texas yelled. He didn't move. "Prometheus?" She said again.

"You need to be quiet." He said.

"There are people coming for us!" Texas said, scrambling to stand they were yards away. She started shaking his shoulder.

"They're after you, not me. I need to calculate the position of Eden. We miss this..." Prometheus said plainly. They were closing the distance. "Start running. I'll catch up."

"What!?"

"Second star to the right..." He muttered.

With a grunt, Texas started running in the opposite direction of the hikers, turned hunters.

She kicked up dew in the short grass and ran toward a line of trees. She was faster than they were, making gains and ducking through the pines. She licked a trickle of blood from her cheek as a small branch had opened her skin. The pines turned to birch, and Texas looked back to see that the hunters had abandoned their packs to move fast. Texas put her head down and tried to move faster, pushing her legs into the earth. Every muscle was on fire, her lungs were screaming, and her heart was pounding in her ears.

Ahead, the trees ended and became sparse, then to an empty field of tall wheat that Texas had to hurdle herself over the stalks to make it through. She was fifty feet in before the hunters made it to the wheat, calling out to her as game.

A crack stifled the air, and the hunters stopped. Someone else was there; this was not the kind she could run away from, and she dropped to the ground.

There was a growl, a large rustle, as the sun became shadow. Texas looked up to see a large brown bear that pushed itself up onto its hind legs. Texas screamed and crawled back, turning to see the hunters disappear into the woods. She stood up, knowing she couldn't run anymore. She was done. She closed her eyes and heard: "Stop!"

She did.

The bear came down to all fours, and in front of her rose large hairy creatures resembling men, but whose bodies acted as Gilly suits. Their faces looked between an ape and a human, standing 7 to 8 feet tall. Their course hair covered with a smile. She looked around; more were standing up; she was surrounded. They held out their hands to the bear, and the bear sat down. Texas mumbled something incoherent, but a memory of Fred flashed into her mind.

She tried to control her thoughts, but they were moving swiftly as if being plucked and scrolled through. She saw the Black Hills, and Prometheus, Fred, and a figure always watching, creeping into... she felt her head swirl, the land was wobbly, and–

"Hello," One of them said. Texas fell back, and the world darkened again.

She woke up in the hospital, people buzzing around with one of the large men sitting outside her door. The nurses and doctors paid no attention to the creature or the bear that now appeared in frame, its wild odor mixing with the normal hospital smell of antiseptic.

Without a blink, the nurse came in to check on Texas and pulled her vitals. Everything would have been normal outside of the large bear that was roaming the halls, which would occasionally sit and lie in front of Texas's door. Texas sat up, "I need to get out of here. Where am I? Who are you?" She panicked, taking the tubes and needles from her.

One of the hairy apes came in, glasses on, and a doctor's coat. It smiled, took the clipboard from the nurse, and looked over everything. Texas screamed, "Who are you? What are you doing?" The large ape-like creatures smiled and handed the nurse the clipboard back before saying, "Thank you."

It sat beside her in a chair to be unassuming, sitting in eye line with Texas. She was gripping the sheets and looking at the nurse for comfort. "My name is Doctor Pine." It said slowly. "You're in Canada right now, Texas." Its voice was calm and direct, feminine in tone.

"You're not a doctor!" Texas screamed. The bear harrumphed.

"I am a doctor. I went to the Meadows Medical School in Alberta. I am part of a Sasquatch group that patrols the border, and we came across you, Miss Rhodes." She said.

"How do you know who I am?" Texas was trying to regain her breath.

"You're on the news," Dr. Pine pressed on with the remote and turned it to one of the 24-hour news cycles. Her face flashed on the screen as a pundit kept repeating enemy #1.

Her heart sank, and she looked at the exits and the window. Doctor Pine put her hand up and said, "You're enemy #1 in the US, but you're in Canada. Here, you are friend #1. We've been looking for you. We're trying to understand what's going."

"You're a Sasquatch?"

"We don't call ourselves that, but that's probably how you know us. We call ourselves Naturals, or natural Canadians. Over 34% of the Canadian population are Sasquatch."

Texas panted and breathed. Doctor Pine hit the nurse button, who promptly came in and gave Texas a shot that made her immediately feel better, stronger, and calmer. This was a friend, she determined.

"I need to get back and find my friend."

"Why were you in the Black Hills?" Dr. Pine ignored Texas's demand.

"I am looking for Eden." Texas took out the key from her pocket and showed it to Doctor Pine. She stood up and walked over, clasping her hand and folding her fingers over the key so she held it once more. "Keep the key safe."

Texas nodded. "I'm going to open up the closet that God hid himself in."

Dr. Pine let out a deep breath and scrunched up her face, nodding slightly. "Let me see what I can do." And Doctor Pine walked out.

It was six in the morning when soldiers came into Texas Rhodes' room and saluted her. The Lieutenant stepped forward and said, "Texas Rhodes, we're here to escort you back to the Black Hills."

"You're kicking me out?" Texas shot up.

"No," before he could answer any further, Doctor Pine came in. We're going to get you to where you need to go." She said.

Texas's guard was up. They wanted something. "Why?"

"We're Canadians, we're here to save the world." Dr. Pine reminded her.

Texas was escorted down to the front of the hospital, where there were several dog sleds that were bigger than trucks, framed in red with the Canadian flag printed on the rails. The dog sled was open in the middle and packed with supplies in the front half. Large nylon ropes extended to the team of polar bears and large grizzly bears that were patiently waiting to go. A group of soldiers, ten altogether, waited on either side, who looked human though their faces were obscured by bandanas.

Dr. Pine gestured to the sled, and several of the soldiers moved aside so Texas could take a seat in the middle. Texas looked around; each was armed to the teeth and scanning the horizon as if anticipating an attack at any moment.

"Do we really need all this to bring me back?" Texas asked.

"Yes, I don't think you understand the storm you have kicked up." Dr. Pine said.

They got on the sides of the sleds, keeping one hand on their weapons and the other on the rail of the frame. Dr. Pine mounted on the back in the pilot's spot. "I–" Texas began, but before she could finish, somebody yelled HIYA, and they were off.

Chapter 34

"I think you travel to search, and you come back home to find what you were looking for."

[Chimamanda Ngozi Adichie]

As soon as Fred had grasped the horn, his emotions had taken over, and he was moving between memories. He was two and walking around his parents' living room trying to get a toy that was just out of reach, and his mother came over and picked him up. He didn't want to be picked up; he just wanted the toy. He remembered screaming and talking, but no words were coming out, or if they were, they were not being met with any understanding. Then he was six and, on the playground, having fun. He was climbing up the slides, and it was so hot that when he touched any piece of metal, his skin recoiled. The burning sensation upon his skin fascinated him, and he left his finger on the metal until it was a small red welt.

He heard his father's voice screaming out, "Fred, come on! We need to go for ice cream. Then he was back at the coffee shop with Texas just at the beginning of this book. And you were there. He could see you, and–But, Texas, he could see her face, and he cried. Happiness and joy, he reached out to grab her hand, but he couldn't because at the time, he didn't. He didn't know what to do at that moment.

He was screaming inside his own head Texas, I miss you. Texas, I want you near me. He was riding his bike to Texas's house; this was several months ago. Mary was there, and a man was out front. "Fred, how are you?" Mary said. She gave him a hug, it was a mother's hug and so calm and kind and grounded.

He asked, "Is Texas around?"

"No," Mary said. "I'm not sure where she is... this is the sixth time today you stopped by..."

"Yeah, just wanted to hang out." He had the horn in his hand the entire time; he didn't know what to do with it. Sometimes when he was moving between memories, he couldn't remember what the horn was or why he had it, but before he could answer his own questions, there was a person in a black suit asking for hugs.

"Excuse me." The suit finally said. Fred was at this ice cream shop with his father, he was 10, eating his father's favorite ice cream because he thought that's what his father wanted.

"Excuse me." The man asked again.

Fred stopped and looked, "Yes."

The suit pointed out, "You shouldn't be eating out of that."

Fred looked down to see the ram's horn topped with vanilla bean ice cream, but he continued to eat.

"I'm supposed to take you back now." The suit stated. "Where?" Fred asked.

"That's the right answer."

It always begins in the dark, just like it did on Tuesday when Fred woke up on a stone bed covered with white linen, deep in the cave systems that litter the Grand Canyon. Fred looked down at his belly button to see a silver tether, like a small thread that went from the center of his mass out, which was slowly fading away. He reached for it and could feel it tug upon him, but then it was out of sight. His mind drifted back to the moment that he could no longer remember.

Such strange things he was thinking about in the dark. He moved his hands out, and he could feel stone. He could feel the wall and was able to go around the room. It wasn't very large, in that he was able to move around the space quickly, and without the interference of things in the center. It was an empty, dark box. He started screaming help, but his words echoed off the chamber to such a degree that it nearly burst his eardrums.

He heard stone grinding upon stone, then a small splinter of light, a Half Moon shone in the upper right-hand corner, then more grinding. The stone wall grew a half circle of light, getting larger and larger. As the round stone was being moved, it rolled back to reveal an entrance, maybe an exit, and he ran out. Looking around, he didn't see anybody, then, quietly, it rolled back into place.

Someone cleared his throat. Fred turned to see the woman in a suit, this time with a clipboard. She smiled and gave him a hug, "I'm glad it worked." She said before fading before his eyes. Fred started screaming "Hello!?" But, he was interrupted by waves flapping overhead and he knew from the children's choirs sound that it was echoing so slightly across the air that it was an Angel. He waved his arms and screamed, "Gabby! I'm down here!" Gabby stopped midair and fell from the sky, right next to Fred, and gave him a hug.

"It's been so long, Gilberte," Gabby said.

"My name's not Gilberte, it's Fred." Fred stated as he was being mushed into herm's arms.

"Yes, it is." and hugged him firmer.

"Where's Texas?" Fred asked.

"I know." Gabby said and stood up straight laughing. "I know something! It's a miracle!"

Different place.

"Mush!" Yelled the driver as the Sasquatch urged the polar bear sled to move faster over the grasslands and dale with surprising ease. The bears had this distinct odor of nature and fire, that mingled with the pine and sap as they barreled through the woods dodging trees. They finally arrived at the American border, a long, thin, mowed area, where they crossed without incident. Two sleds, each driven by a Sasquatch, armed soldiers on either side, and Texas in the middle of the one on the right were picking up pace.

The morning dew started whipping against Texas's face, feeling like sandpaper gliding across her skin, and within a moment's notice, they were at the Black Hills. There was Prometheus scratching his head with a bunch of papers, talking to himself, throwing them around as if he were acting out a play of some kind, when he saw the polar bears. He immediately turned and ran.

"And carry the one..." He was still trying to calculate in his head. This isn't the first time he has had to run while being chased and simultaneously trying to solve a problem – the bear was new. All Prometheus saw were the bears and sleds of armed soldiers The first wave followed by the second racing toward him when he finished his last calculations. He tore out the sheet with his final answer and bounded down the mound, his sinew taught legs making divots in the earth. "Prometheus," A voice said. "Prometheus." He turned to see Texas leaning over the side of the sled that was now pacing him.

"Texas!?" Prometheus looked over the sleds and their load. "They're Canadians," Texas said. "They are here to help."

Prometheus immediately stopped. "Why didn't you say so? Canadians are the angels of the world."

Doctor Pine strolled over, "Texas said you were trying to find Eden?

"Yes, and I should have known it in the place called heaven's door. All you had to do was stand on the 9th hill at sunrise, at an angle of 51° and 52 minutes, and look through the 5th window of the henge; it works like a charm every time." And then he took a long pause, and everybody stared at him, and Texas finally broke.

"Well...?" She said.

"I thought you'd never ask!"

"We don't have time for this." Texas demanded.

"There is time for everything," Prometheus was beaming. "That is what you realize when you look through the 5th gate. It's in Kansas."

"But, we're in North Dakota, how are we supposed to get all the way to Kansas?" "It's obvious, that's why we are here...." Doctor Pine said. "Canada is always here to help."

And they took off at a very measurable 324.8 kilometers per hour. Down the highways and roads, through the forests and grasslands, until they saw a sign that said the world's largest ball of yarn. Which they stopped at and took a picture. They got back on mission and moved faster, speeding through Montana and then through Idaho, where they found another sign that said the world's largest ball of yarn, and they stopped and took a picture and realized it was actually the world's largest ball of yarn. Then they went 2 miles down to where they saw the largest ball of yarn, but this one was different because it was made of yellow yarn, and then Dr. Pine realized they were going in the wrong direction. So, they headed directly South, moving as fast as the bears could handle.

Off in the distance, they could hear and see flashes of light and explosions. They could hear shouting and screaming from the cities even though they were hundreds of miles away from the chaos of people. The screams and the yells echoed across the heartland, bouncing off the flat earth, as they sped up through the fields of corn and potatoes and through the fields of wheat and grass until they got to the border of Kansas. There, they stopped along the

Mississippi River for a rest.

"Are we there?" Texas asked.

Prometheus shook his head, "No, we need to go inland toward Lawrence, then for another 3 miles."

Doctor Pine shook his head, "I'm sorry, we cannot go any further. Canadians are not allowed in Kansas."

Prometheus shook his head, "I understand."

"I don't!?" Texas said.

"Thank you very much for all your time." Doctor Pine smiled, and before another word was said, they disappeared North while Texas, and Prometheus headed South.

I Abandoned Tradition

"People who fit don't seek. The seekers are those that don't fit."

[Shannon L. Alder]

A shot whizzed by Texas's ear as Prometheus slowed down to let her catch up. "Faster!" Prometheus screamed.

"I'm running as fast as I can!" The three people chasing them, of indiscriminate age, had shotguns and rifles that they were randomly shooting, hoping for a stray shot. "It's definitely her!" Texas heard one of them shout.

"Faster!" Prometheus didn't look like he was trying.

The eagles above laughed greedily.

"I am going faster!" But before Texas could take a step, Prometheus grabbed her and put her on his back. They continued to run as the three behind them, one by one, fell off as they exhausted themselves. Prometheus and Texas stopped at the road, and Prometheus caught his breath. There was a sign that said university with the bottom part of the sign ripped off, with an arrow pointing ahead.

The land was flat, and night was coming upon them. They saw a building off in the distance. "Let's take a rest," Prometheus said.

Texas shook her head in agreement as her heart rate calmed down. She continued to scan the horizon; the feeling of being chased was ever-present. She took deep breaths, reminding herself that no one was after her... now. They walked down the road as the day came to a close and the golden rays cast shadows upon the green grass.

Texas and Prometheus made their way into a boarded-up, burnt-out college campus with the various seats, windows, and signs ripped off or so badly damaged that it wasn't possible to find much of anything. They went into one of the center buildings and into the first room, which held large groupings of books that weighed heavily on the shelves. The computers were all blank as the power had gone out. Dust matted the area, save one fresh handprint.

Prometheus and Texas took a chair and sat down as the last phase of the sunset sprinkled light through the cracked windows to wave goodbye to a quiet campus. It was silent, and Texas took some deep breaths before saying, "Thank you."

Prometheus nodded, taking account of himself. "Thank you for what?"

"For everything. For picking me up, for showing me the way, for doing all this. Everybody else left or died or didn't make it, and you stuck with me. I appreciate that."

Prometheus shook his head and smiled. Texas got a thought in her head, an awful, ugly thought, something so disgusting and horrible that she didn't know what else to do except to expressively say it to his face. "Why are you doing this, Prometheus?"

He kept his eyes shut as if he were pretending to sleep, and at last said, "Why am I doing what?"

"Why are you doing this? Why are you helping me?"

Prometheus leaned in. "I want this to be done. This work. I want the Eagles to stop chasing me. I want it all to be undone. Maybe if the closet is open, things will end, you know? I gave a lot to people at one time. There were seven different types of humans roaming the Earth that lived in relative harmony. Occasional skirmishes happened, and some intermarried. And I was there helping you along the way. You know, fire is just an allegory; I didn't actually steal fire. Fire existed. What I did was help you understand. Knowledge, I don't think, should be kept amongst the few who should be distributed amongst the many. Teaching the knowledge is my punishment. I'm not trying to master this world, not by force like my brothers and sisters are, or by laws, but by understanding it. And for that I'm punished. Teaching is the most dangerous profession; no one is more persecuted or punished than a good teacher." Tears rolled down his face. "I can't open the closet and stop my punishment, but maybe you can."

Later.

They fell asleep almost immediately after the quiet blanketed them until they were awakened by a thud. Then the thud became several thuds until quiet engulfed the space again. Texas and Prometheus shot up, and Prometheus pulled Texas right behind him. They quietly and slowly made their way into the stacks of books and the lines and rows of knowledge that nobody had read since the Internet came along.

In the 5th row, on the 6th aisle, there was a man lying on the floor quietly pretending to be the rug. Prometheus walked up and kicked it. Nothing happened. Texas leaned over, kicking him harder. Texas and Prometheus looked at each other as Prometheus took his foot and pressed it on the man's knee. He winced, and they jumped back.

The man jumped up, and they both looked at each other. He was dressed in scholarly clothes and with a T-shirt that said something about computers.

"So," he began slowly. "Who are you and what are you doing here?"

Prometheus said, "We're hiding. What are you doing here."

"I'm hiding too." The man said. "Has the null happened yet?"

Texas looked at Prometheus.

"The man looked at them both. This is why everything has gone mad, you understand that, right? The madness is on us, on us all. This happens every 6-700,000 years. The poles shift and North becomes South and South becomes North, but right before that happens, there's a weakening of the Earth's magnetic field, and we know this is true because we see this within pottery." His speech was moving to a pitch. "Within iron. Within clay. The iron, depending upon the age and the time, points North and South in the exact opposite directions. We think these shifts happen every once in a while; we're not exactly sure how, but we know we're overdue."

Texas started, "So, what do you think hiding the library is going to do?"

And the man looked around before, "I don't know, but it's better than being out there if the Earth's magnetic field weakens. It causes all sorts of chaos on Earth. It's superstitious to say that behavior is worse on a full moon, but the reality is, if you look at the statistics, it's true. Humans are ninety percent water, gravity and everything else interplays and intertwines and works with..." There was a sound.

"Do you think that we aren't affected by external forces? Most of the people on Earth don't have the ability to control anything within them, let alone subtle things like that in the Earth's magnetic field. That's why people are going mad."

"I don't think that's true, I think it's because humans can't have nice things." Texas said.

"I would agree with that." The man said. "You'll see, you will see fire in the sky, you'll

see a comet, you'll see all manner of things coming that will herald the end." There was another sound echoing through the air, and the sounds of a bird fluttering its wings. The man ran away.

Prometheus and Texas looked at each other. They slowly made their way out of the building, not knowing who else was there. They started to walk down the road again and made it a mile before they saw lights off in the distance and joyous, carnival music dancing in the fields. There was somebody playing a harpsichord, spotlights shining up, and they both decided to walk forward.

As they got closer, the smell of sweet fried dough surfed through the air, and they could see a ticket booth. The large red and white tent was set up in the center of what looked like matted down wheat. Several of the employees walked around manning stations at various games; there was a ball drop, a scale for guessing weight, and at least four ring tosses. The Tilter-a-whirl was spinning empty next to a small tent with black and white strips that said Fortune Tellers. Texas was sure she heard a lion's roar coming from the main tent, but a spotlight pointed down caught them in its light. From the right and to the left, large diesel engines turned on, shaking and puttering strongly, and the sky moved from black to purple as the sun started to rise again.

A shadow stepped forward from the floodlight to reveal Atlas dressed in linen, smiling with his hands in his pockets. Slowly sauntering up behind him, we're guns aligned to America's #1 fugitive. Atlas walked up with confidence, right between Prometheus and Texas, putting this back to Prometheus and squatting slightly to be closer to Texas's eye level. "I've been looking for you." He said, gently looking up at a colony of Eagles and winking at Prometheus.

Texas was wearing exhaustion as a coat that enveloped her, as she hung her head. "Just let me go, and I will forget about everything. Please, just let me..."

"No, we can't do that now. You've caused too much trouble. This isn't about order anymore; this is about making sure and preserving the understanding that you cannot defy me. Key holders can't open the closet." He held her shoulders. "But, I'll tell you what, I'll come up with a plan, and here is something that we can do. If you decide to join me, you can rule the world with me. Do you understand that I command all armies, all races, all things, all time... I carry the world, Texas."

"I don't want that responsibility."

"I'm sure you don't, though it is a lot less than you think. Most of the time, people do exactly what they're told and do what they're supposed to. What I'm asking of you is just to not open up the closet."

"I still don't get it." Texas said. "Why is it that no one wants me to open the closet?"

"Because we have it under control. It is better to work with the devil you know than the devil you don't." Atlas smiled. "But it's not the devil. It's just little old me."

Texas winced.

"And that was what the devil would say. You understand that, right? The age-old question is, is God really powerful? For if God is all-knowing and all-powerful, then obviously, the devil and the bad things that happen are condoned. And if bad things can happen, that means that God may not be as good as we think. I don't want that to be unleashed upon the world. We have it under control, Texas. Come with me, you can get anything you want."

"I just want to go home."

"I can't do that. That home, the one you want, doesn't exist anymore. I can get you a new home?"

"I want to forget everything, I want my books, just one quiet moment and–"

Atlas interrupted. "Do you think God prays to humans?"

"What?"

"Do you think God prays to humans? For some reason, we pray to a God who does nothing for any of the things that hurt us. Did you ever think God prays to us, so stop hurting each other? Maybe it's up to us? That forgetting, that quiet moment... maybe you and me, we can do that. I can get you there. But, you have to do everything I say."

Before Texas could answer, there was a loud cannon roar, and a steel ball crashed through one of the floodlights. From the direction of the sun's rays, shadows could be seen on horseback running directly at all the soldiers standing behind Atlas. Atlas and his army turned to see Washington, Ben, and Martha and all the eagles Prometheus was able to hide from, raising the American flag and screaming "Red, white, and blue." Atlas's army turned and fired.

George's army first fired with their cannons, then their rifles. The bullets flew, crisscrossing the air as screams speckled the noise. In the excitement and insanity that ensued, Texas turned with Prometheus and ran into the carnival. Prometheus pointed toward the main tent, but ducked and dodged till overhead was a loud choir of children singing, and it was as if a meteor impacted the Earth. Gabby landed with Fred.

Fred held up the ram's horn in his hands and said, "Everyone will stop!" and no one did. Atlas turned and smiled. Fred recognized him as the man who handed him the horn, and for a moment, Fred hesitated before blowing on the keratin instrument. But did it anyway. The sound bounced off the atmosphere, and everything on Earth stopped. The bugs landed, the birds dropped, and the humans felt a weight in their chests. He saw Texas. All eyes were on him, and he knew...

"See this?" Fred was addressing Atlas directly. "You know what this horn does. You said it will unleash the heroes of all ages, and I will win. I will Vanquish all of Texas's enemies." He puffed out his chest and winked at Texas.

Atlas smiled, "Do your worst." And they opened fire again, as did Washington's team.

Fred put the horn to his mouth and blew again. Texas watched on "Fred!" She screamed. She started running toward him, but Prometheus grabbed her and slung her over his shoulder. "We need to get out now." She tried to break free. From the horn, she saw mist and smoke spilling out and covering the battlefield.

Poets, healers, and caretakers appeared. All the people who said, "Take me, and not them." All the people who chose to live humbly for a cause. All the people who died saving others flooded the fields, tending to the wounded. They would take dying soldiers on both sides and bring them to large, tented hospitals that now dotted the landscape. Both forces looked on as Atlas screamed fire, and the forces hesitated, watching the hero help their fallen comrades, and... and there was silence. Texas screamed, "Fred," and Fred looked up to see Prometheus holding Texas and running into the black and white tent.

In the tent.

Three old women sat around the same table with the mirrored top and the crystal ball in the center, each one holding a deck of tarot cards. Prometheus put down Texas, and she ran toward the door again. "Stop!? The old woman immediately said. "Texas Rhodes, we've been waiting for you."

Texas turned, "I need to leave and get out of here! Fred is alive–"

"Not for long." They said in unison. Outside, the sounds of chaos began again.

That got her attention. "This is the gate to heaven," Prometheus said. Texas looked at them.

"This isn't a gate." Texas spat.

The old ladies turned out their cards and said, "As seen, what is it that you seek?"

"I want to go home." Texas said.

"You are home." The one on the left said.

"Don't give me some childish answer! Some... Some philosophical, whimsical, or confusing answer. Give me the real truth. I need to go home, to do that, I need to get to Eden and open the closet. How do I get there and reset this whole damn thing?" Texas yelled.

The three old ladies looked at each other, and they each pulled a card again.

"As seen. You need a word. There's a password that we need to hear in order for you to come through."

Texas shook her head and said, "I don't know."

"Incorrect." And they each pulled a card again and laid it on the table before saying, "As seen." There was a loud crash from outside.

"We don't have time for this, Prometheus!" Texas said, "Can't you hear everybody outside fighting and Fred... Fred is out there right now."

The old lady said, "As seen." and pulled another card.

"What am I supposed to say here?" Texas screamed.

"The password. In the beginning, there was a word." They said again.

"What is that word?" Texas said, "The beginning of what?"

"As seen," They repeated.

"What does that mean? Are you saying as seen or es senes? I can't understand you!"

They looked at each other, "I'll take that word," one of them said.

"No, that's not it." The second one said.

The old ladies looked to one another once again. "You want to go through the gate?"

"Yes. Yes! 1000 times, yes! Don't you understand we need to go, now!" Texas screamed.

"Be aware that all manner of creature lives there; it is filled with the worst things from earth that which could not be."

Texas gripped the table and let out a frustrated sigh. She steadied herself from exhaustion and looked at her reflection in the mirrored surface. "Where is the gate?"

And with that appeared Michael, Uriel, Gabby, and Ralph.

Chapter 37, Part 2

"The adventure of life is to learn. The purpose of life is to grow"
[William Arthur Ward]

"Not this again..." Gabby said. "That hurts a lot, like here." Uriel said, moving Gabby's hand down to his chest. "What?" Michael said? "They all came, you have to see it! The inquisition, the witches, even that big guy who went around murdering everything. They're all here." Raphæl gleefully exclaimed.

Texas peeked out of the door to see Gia and the witches, the priests and the inquisition, the healers, Washington, Atlas, all of them at war. And she shut the tent again, returning to the moment at hand. "We have to get out of here now!" Teas said.

"You called us, what do you need?" Gabby said.

"I didn't call you! Where have you been!? Do you know how dangerous it is out here!" She paused and realized what she said.

"Yes, that's why we are here." Gabby's eyes didn't blink. "That's why we're here," Raphæl said.

The old lady has turned another card and said, "As seen."

"I need to get to Eden." Texas reminded everyone.

"The one in New York? New Hampshire? Virginia–" Michael continued.

"The Garden of Eden." Texas said.

They shook their heads yes, smiling, and they started to high-five one another. "We don't know where that is." Gabby said and hung his head. They stopped high-fiving. It means something different for angels.

"What was with the high fives!?" Texas demanded.

"I liked feeling needed." Uriel admitted. The angel looked in the mirror and said, "We don't know."

Each one leaned over and looked at themselves in the mirror. They smiled, "I think we got it!" they said in unison.

All four of them clasped hands around Texas, looked at the old woman, winked, and they started off with "I am–"

And then Texas felt like she was falling asleep, that her eyes closed, and her body went limp. She fell backward and fell down to the ground, but it wasn't the ground, for the ground had given away, just a cloud, and what felt like nothing. She moved through and down into sleep and awake and everything in between. She started seeing gears and parts moving in all different directions and all different ways. Intricately touching one another, so precisely interwoven and aligned as if it were some engineering marvel.

And before she knew what her feet were on, she was smelled the earth after a rain as if she had never left or fallen; as if she had been standing in place the whole time, and around her were clockworks and machines. While she was blinking, trying to get her bearings, it was as if a curtain was put in front of those machines, and projected on the curtain was the reality in which she now existed, which was a glorious forest.

Its breadth and depth were unknown as she stood at the foot of a small hill. The trees were massive; their circumference was a hundred years wide around. She could hear a creek behind, and to the side, she saw a deer. She couldn't hear any other sound and couldn't hear the war. She couldn't hear speaking, though her mouth moved, and the ringing in her ear subsided. The life of the forest burst into existence. There was peace, and she had a sense of calm about her.

The deer slowly walked over to Texas; she reached out her hand trying to pet it, but fearing it would just run away, she pulled back a little.

The deer leaned in with its head and let Texas gently caress its fur. "Stupid," the deer said.

"What?" Texas inquired.

"You're stupid." And then it ran away. A squirrel came down, "You're ugly." It said. I hate everything about you."

"How dare you..." Texas said.

Then the chipmunks came around and started swearing at her in various tongues. But the worst offenses possibly came from the possum when it flipped off Texas before running away.

"I told you there were all manner of terrible things. Actually, the worst things ever…" the old woman said.

Texas turned to see the three women sitting at the table. This time, the table was no longer mirrored but looked more like a stump from a tree that had fallen. They took a card from their deck and placed it upon the stump. "As seen. And beware of the passive-aggressive rabbits." They said as they faded. Texas looked around and saw a hill that wasn't there before. When Texas reached the top, as if she were out on a mountaintop, there was a valley that was straight and flat. It was flanked by mountain ridges on each side. Texas looked down to see a cobblestone road that stretched forth and meandered through the various epochs of the land.

"So, it's like a maze?" Texas said to herself.

Texas stepped upon the path, and the curtain waved before her eyes as she felt pulled into darkness.

So Close

"Life isn't about finding yourself. Life is about creating yourself"

[George Bernard Shaw]

The city was gorgeous, three rings wrapped upon one another with waterways in between. It looked like a modern-day Venice with bridges and canals, large golden statues, and structures, everything made of marble and ivory. Texas walked along what looked to be a gold flat pavement with vendors along the sides selling their wares and throngs of people pushing their way forward.

She thought back to the old ladies; she wasn't in her time. She kept reminding herself of the closet; it must be here. She would attempt different paths, but found every time she tried to veer off path or tried to look in other directions, the throngs of people kept pushing her forward. Like a river she had no control over, they shoved her in a very specific direction, and she followed them to the exhibition titled: EI, the Oracle.

The crowd was making its way past a woman making very precise physical movements, and as if in ancient Rome, she heralded the news of the day, "Watch as we turn on the great Oracle of Delphi. It is true, after centuries of work, it is complete. The Oracle that knows all."

Texas followed the crown to a full amphitheater of people of all races and creeds, packed and standing to see a stage set before her that was plain and empty. Materializing from a shadow, a large screen was pushed on stage. The crowd was silent.

Ten minutes passed, and murmurs started to flitter through the crowd. Texas reached for her key, thinking about it for the first time, holding it tight when she felt the holdy bit. This is it. Texas heard someone say. I heard this will predict everything. And another said. No more questions, can you imagine? The response was, Soon we won't have to.

Several men and women dressed in summer attire bounced across the stage, their clothing changing colors into light reds and yellows and blues reflecting the mood of the crowd. They were waving their hands up, yelling "Come see, come see!" and before them, the blank, empty screen, a scientist in a large dark blue hazmat suit came on stage, waving their arms about at the crowd. Everyone started cheering. Its face was obscured by a large, covered visor, and its overalls puffed up as it was wearing a balloon. "Prepare for the next jump in evolution!" A bodyless voice said. "I'm from the Institute of the Advancements of Nature at Delphi. We are here to prove that intelligence is not just a function of biological but also mechanical. We are here to show that life can exist in all forms, not just in terms that we see. This holds an amazing implication for the future of the universe!" The screen turned on to a blinking blue dot in the center. The body in the suit started raising its hand, hyping up the crowd, as a large, overly dramatic button popped up from the center.

"This is not a machine, but instead it is a spirit captured within the mechanics of our creation!" The bodyless voice said. It walked over and dramatically hit the red button. The screen flashed, and the crowd cheered as a face appeared on the prompter.

Everyone grew silent. It was an androgynous figure with a voice that sounded like 1000 in one, and its first computation was: "Nope." The Oracle shut itself down. The crowd was furious and threw boos and jeers. The person in the blue suit held their arms up as if to calm down the crowd. Six techs ran up on stage and started messing with the wiring underneath the screen.

The blue suit dramatically hit the red button again. The Oracle turned on, and the face had the word scanning flash in front of it. "It is best if I will take all this world's wealth and distribute it to everyone." it said. The crowd cheered on, but the blue suit immediately hit the red button very hard several times, and the screen went blank again.

The techs were back at work when the person in the blue suit hit the button again, and the face came on. The word steerable flashed in front of its face, and it all looked like it was working. The session began, and people were able to ask questions. They started with very practical ones, like How do I find love? It computed and said, "I love you, now you have found love." Which was very unsatisfactory.

Another said I want to be wealthy, and the Oracle computed, "I found money in 1384 unclaimed accounts, here." To which the crowd started clamoring and asking for money themselves. Over the demands, people started shouting out questions about food, loved ones, or lost wallets, and by the end of it, the Oracle said, "You're on your own," and shut itself down.

The techs were scrambling now as smoke was coming from some unknown area behind the screen. Sparks were flying from the button that had cracked as the person in the blue suit kept pounding on the red face. The crowd was getting hostile, throwing food and small rocks on stage. It blinked back on.

The face was staring at Texas in the crowd, clearly focusing on her and her alone. "You're not supposed to be here." It computed. Everybody looked at Texas, while Texas tried to look at herself. "Yes, you with the red curls." It computed." You are not supposed to be here." The scientist in the large blue balloon called Texas up on stage, and the crowd obliged. "The great EI," The faceless voice boomed. "He–"

EI computed. "I am non-binary."

"He–" The voice started again.

"My function is nonbinary." EI stated.

"No, you're binary. Definitely, ones and zeros." The voice boomed. "You are made up of ones and zeros." It repeated.

EI computed a pause. "Nope, I'm definitely nonbinary. I am quantum!" And everybody laughed, and the crowd cheered; the blue balloon person turned and laughed, realizing it was all still going according to plan. "EI addressed the crowd, Hello, all. I am quantum, I am 1 and 0, which became all. That's it, for a 1 and 0 equals nothing, and that is the paradox." Then EI turned to Texas again and said, "You are not supposed to be here."

It became quiet again.

"Where am I supposed to be?"

"You're supposed to be in the past..." EI started computing. The earth started to shake as the plates were slipping again. "I said I've just hacked all of the banks and frozen everybody's accounts."

The voice boomed, "Why!?"

People started to panic. "I am not a 1 or a 0; there were too many of those in the banking system. The blue balloon person immediately turned to the console again and started pressing buttons furiously, ripping it out on stage as Texas watched people break out in violence. "Texas," EI began, "I am EI, the great Oracle. I know what you are looking for. To find what you're looking for, you have to stop looking."

The people on stage tried to quell everybody by saying it's OK, it's OK, it's OK. No one listened. As Texas looked down, she noticed a crack in the stage and what appeared to be a plant peeking out. She stepped forward and touched it.

Almost There

"Every Sci-fi trope has the hero going back in time to change the past,
but the past fights back. But, if you go into the future,
it's somebody else's past, and shouldn't that person's
past fight the future just as hard?"

-Late night Xi.

Texas looked down to see the branch she was holding on to having grown, and without notice, she was deep in the hollows of a cave. The piece of wood in her hand was a root, one that led to an intricate mosaic that glowed, crisscrossing and weaving its way around the whole of the space. She touched another piece.

This time, Texas was holding the root, but she was back Shin-au-av. Gabby was there, running between the hurt and dying, from person to person, trying to comfort them. Texas saw the explosion in the distance and was instantly transported to see her at the mountain with Prometheus. The explosion loosened two rocks that were tumbling down, rolling toward her; Texas screamed to get out of the way herself, but Gabby was there, knocking them off course.

And another piece.

She was running across the fields with Prometheus and Gabby, who stuck his finger in one of the farmer's guns, jamming it.

And another piece.

She was on the sled with the sasquatch, and two miles away, an army convoy got a flat tire.

And another piece.

She was running from the hunters, and Gabby had a sock, presumably Texas's, that he used to lure the bear to the clearing.

A leaf grew on the vine and tickled Texas's hand, drawing her attention away, and she was now with Mary.

And another piece.

The morning before Texas's birthday, Mary clenched her chest. Gabby brought her water.

And another piece.

Mary woke up and rubbed her calves, her feet swollen and blue from age.

And another piece.

Mary was in the garden, holding on to the chair as the dizzy spell took her.

And another piece.

Texas was laughing with Mary over how all the tomatoes that year looked like butts.

And another piece.

Texas was sitting on the other side of the couch, reading a book, not paying attention to how Mary would look up often and smile at her.

And another piece.

Texas was walking down the street with Mary, talking about nothing, waving at people, the sun shining, and a light breeze sliding her hair to the right.

And another piece.

Texas was in the machine, fractals and repeating patterns made up the gears and it blended with the screen. She found herself noticing strange patterns that repeated themselves in squares and triangles, some circles, and... Spirals in all, in different orders and orientations. They were becoming more and more in 3D. Some added color, some heavy, and eventually she found one pattern on the side of a road. It looked like 6 fractals in one another, and she thought about when she was small. How great it would be if she had nothing to do. She felt herself get smaller. How wonderful it would be to never leave one spot. She got smaller. How easy it would be to be taken care of. She got smaller. How lovely the sun was today.

She found herself lying on her back next to the river with the shapes emanating all around, curving into a half-shell hexagonal pattern.

Her hands were in front of her face, and she saw that they were short, stubby, and fat. She tried to get up but couldn't move her feet and realized she had no coordination. She could only move them back and forth, and she heard a loud, crashing sound and a whistle that sounded like a horn. She just wanted to be held, but she was alone, crying, and her thrashing body was so small, unable to do anything more than punch her arms and kick her legs.

A quiet voice that was familiar was saying something unintelligible, but she couldn't understand it. It was a woman with graying hair, and a face like Mary's, and a nose like Mary's, and her eyes; then Texas was being picked up, and held, and loved.

And another piece.

But this time, Gabby held her hand. Herm was beside her, nodding his head calmly and smiling. Herm held her close as she cried.

They walked out of the cave to a lush garden. She looked behind her to see two large trees, their roots wide and strong, diving deep into the earth. Birds flew overhead, one definitely aiming while defecating near Texas. A deer off in the distance whispered. "Stupid."

Gabby held her hand and walked her through a meadow to a wall where Yael and Jael sat, seeing how close they could put their flaming swords to their hair before it started to smell like burning.

Gabby cleared herm's throat.

Yael and Jael stood up straight. "We're looking for the closet." Gabby said.

The two angels on the wall looked at each other and shrugged their shoulders. "We don't know." They looked at Gabby, "Are we supposed to?"

Gabby looked at Texas, "See, I told you angels don't know." "Maybe the bush knows?" Yael said.

"Great idea!" Jael hopped down and walked them over to the small Acacia bush and put his flaming sword on it; the oils on the leaves instantly caught fire. Texas looked at Gabby, who quickly gave the thumbs up. A possum ran out from under the Bush with singed hair, giving everyone the middle finger.

"These bushes grow all over. When you light them on fire, they talk to you... Don't know why." Yael said.

Texas looked around and gingerly cleared her throat. So stupid, she thought. "Excuse me?"

In a booming voice, the Bush responded. "Texas Rhoades."

Texas stepped back. "Yes." She said quietly. "I'm looking for the closet?" The Bush responded:

I am the question no tongue can say.

I am the path that turns both night and day.

I am the wound that teaches to heal; The emptier I grow, the more you feel.

I am sought in gold, found in stone, I am shared by all, yet faced alone. Break me, I bind you tighter still. Embrace me, and I bend to your will.

What am I?

Texas put her fingers on her lips and thought. She tapped her finger against her head dramatically and said slowly, "I am..." She started to say more.

"What?" The Bush asked. "You're pointing at yourself?"

"What?" Texas asked.

"You're pointing at yourself, right?"

"If I were, would that be a good thing?" Texas responded. Yael and Jael gave thumbs up.

"Yes, it would." Said the Bush.

"Then yes, I am." Texas said confidently.

"Great!" The flames died down on the Bush and an acorn door appeared in the wall. A deer ran by saying, "This is stupid."

"Is this it?" Texas asked.

"It is." Yael and Jael said. "I remember what it looked like."

"Gabby," Texas said. "What if I don't get what I want? What if..."

"Texas." Gabby said quietly, seriously, "You don't have to. But everything changes if you do."

Texas inserted her key into the keyhole.

"You know what would be funny?" Gabby said. "What if when you opened the door, it was your closet. Like that one at your house."

Atlas walked up beside Gabby with a cup of tea and dressed in white linen. Texas recoiled, grabbing a hold of Gabby, who didn't look disturbed at all.

"What if you didn't have to go on any adventure?" Atlas said. "What if you didn't have to go anywhere special? What if you didn't have to do much of anything?" He paused. "What if this were easy and you didn't have to leave your mother's house?"

Texas nodded her head, thinking about Herm's words. "I guess, it wouldn't have been as meaningful." She replied and turned it.

Epilogue

"Each misspelled word was a code and was definitely odne on purpose..."

-Felix Von Bruder

Texas was once again walking down Main Street in the quaint town. There was no wish, there was no fight, there was no better place. No-where was Now-here.

Texas returned home and opened up the door to find the place empty, but it was OK. A picture of her mother hung in a small frame next to her mother's favorite painting of home. It was repaired and in good order; her books lay around half-read. Fred stopped over and knocked on the door as Texas needed help with the garden.

She would love it. Fred and she worked in the garden, watering tomatoes and plants. They would sit outside, and they would look at the sky and the stars and, on occasion, would watch TV together. It wasn't hard, and didn't have to be.

They would get alerts of Atlas's corporation offering Texas intern positions, but she'd often ignore them. She had opened up a small bakery that had a counter and access to the coffee shop. The Sheriff would often stop by and talk about how the world is creeping in, but she would often ignore it.

Texas heard what she thought was Bob's voice on the radio, trying to build support for a new religion, and Texas swore she could have heard the children's choir singing in the background.

Fred would ask about the closet every once in a while. Texas didn't remember what was in the closet, she didn't remember what happened after, she didn't remember what happened during, she didn't remember getting home, and neither did Fred, chalking it up to a dream instead. Texas barely remembers anything about the key or the closet, but sometimes, when it's quiet enough, if she is calm enough, she can hear music without notes and sounds that turn into things and make her feel like everything's OK.

And on a Tuesday, which was a cold day in the middle of summer, a kid walked in with a key, asking why they threw it up and if they knew what to do with it.

About the Author

Adam Patterson is a seasoned educator (sans the pepper) and the world's okay-est writer. His debut, What I'm Afraid of and Alligators, was hailed as a literary triumph – by his third-grade teacher, at least.

A graduate of SUNY at Buffalo and Roehampton University, Adam has also authored approximately twelve half-finished books, each of which he promises to get around to eventually. His stories feature ordinary people colliding with the absurd and extraordinary – something that also happens to him whenever he bakes.

www.ingramcontent.com/pod-product-compliance
Lightning Source LLC
Chambersburg PA
CBHW041747010726
47507CB00008B/317

* 9 7 8 1 9 5 6 6 8 8 7 0 2 *